By Kris Tualla:

Loving the Norseman
Loving the Knight
In the Norseman's House

A Nordic Knight in Henry's Court
A Nordic Knight of the Golden Fleece
A Nordic Knight and his Spanish Wife

A Discreet Gentleman of Discovery
A Discreet Gentleman of Matrimony
A Discreet Gentleman of Consequence
A Discreet Gentleman of Intrigue
A Discreet Gentleman of Mystery

Leaving Norway
Finding Sovereignty
Kirsten's Journal

A Woman of Choice
A Prince of Norway
A Matter of Principle

The Norsemen's War: Enemies and Traitors
The Norsemen's War: Battles Abroad
The Norsemen's War: Finding Norway

An Unexpected Viking
A Restored Viking
A Modern Viking

*****

A Primer for Beginning Authors
Becoming an Authorpreneur

Finding Norway

THE NORSEMEN'S WAR

Book 3:
Kyle & Dahl

Kris Tualla

Kris Tualla

Finding Norway: The Norsemen's War is a work of fiction. Names, characters, places and incidents are products of the author's imagination or are used fictitiously and are not to be construed as real. Any resemblance to actual events, locales, organizations, or persons, living or dead, is entirely coincidental.

Published in the United States of America.

© 2016 by Kris Tualla

All rights reserved. No part of this book may be used or reproduced in any form or by any means without the prior written consent of the Publisher, except for brief quotations used in critical articles or reviews.

ISBN-13: 978-1542306003
ISBN-10: 1542306000

*This book is dedicated to the
wives and mothers of our
brave soldiers no matter which war
their husbands and sons
fought in.*

CHAPTER ONE

July 2, 1950
Arendal, Norway

Kyle held five-year-old Thor's hand as they got off the bus in the town square of Arendal. The two days of travel, flying from Minneapolis to Oslo, spending the night in a hotel, then taking the four hour bus ride to her late husband's ancestral home were as exhausting as they were intimidating.

What if they don't like me?

Little Thor had come through like a champ, fascinated by every aspect of the journey, and his dual citizenship with Norway and America made that part easy.

Kyle furtively looked over the people in the square while the bus driver unloaded their two large suitcases, wondering if Teigen Hansen remembered that he needed to pick her up.

"Thank you," she said to the driver. "We'll be fine."

At least I speak Norsk.

Making this trip was important to Tor, who in his active-duty survivor's letter asked Kyle to please stay in contact with his family and take his son to meet them. The fact that she was full-blooded Norwegian but had never visited her own ancestral land made the journey all the more poignant.

"Where's my uncle?" Thor asked in English as the bus pulled away from the square.

Kyle wished she'd been able to teach him Norsk, but with completing her bachelor's degree in psychology at the University of Minnesota and starting her master's program, she'd been far too busy.

Maybe I should have looked for a roommate who also spoke Norwegian.

It was too late now.

"He's on his way," Kyle said with a confidence she didn't own. "We'll just wait right here. Isn't this a nice town?"

It truly was.

Picturesque and sitting on the island-strewn southern coast of Norway, Arendal was protected from the North Sea by a multitude of rocky outcroppings. Tor explained that with Denmark only ninety miles across the water from Arendal this was a perfect location for his Viking ancestors to settle in—and later for his family's long-standing shipping business to thrive.

Kyle heaved a nervous sigh.

What if they don't like me?

She shaded her eyes from the bright summer sun and scanned the square again. Then she gasped. Her free hand pressed against her mouth. Her heart pounded against her ribs.

A ghost was walking toward her.

"Kyle?"

Now that he was close enough she could see his bright green eyes. Not blue, green.

She nodded. "I'm sorry. I just…" Tears blurred her vision. "Tor always said you looked alike."

Teigen smiled his surprised understanding. "I didn't think about that. I guess it would be a shock."

"Mamma?" Thor's face was twisted in concern. "What's wrong."

Kyle quickly wiped her eyes. "Nothing darling. I'm just happy to meet your Uncle Teigen."

Thor looked up at his tall uncle. "You look like my Pappa."

"Do you know any English?" Kyle asked Teigen after she

translated her son's comment.

"A little." Teigen squatted down so his eyes were level with Thor's. "And you are same as your Pappa," he managed in heavily-accented English.

"Everybody says that." Thor pulled his hand from Kyle's and held it out to Teigen. "It's nice to meet you, Uncle Teigen."

Teigen laughed, sounding so much like his older brother that Kyle's chest tightened.

He grabbed Thor's hand and shook it. "It's nice to meet you, Thor Hansen."

Then he straightened and looked down at Kyle. "Shall we go?"

ᚾ ᚾ ᚾ

Hansen Hall was built on the top of a bluff about a mile west of the center of Arendal. Looking exactly like Tor described, the structure was dominated by a round stone tower which stood three stories over the road. There were no windows in the tower, only the vertical slits which allowed archers to defend the inhabitants.

Viking archers.

Extending off one side of the tower was the two-story medieval structure with glass windows leaded in a multitude of small diamond-shaped panes. Peeking over the flat roof of the medieval façade were several tall chimneys and slanted slate roofs declaring the presence of the "modern" wing—built over two hundred years ago.

Kyle climbed out of the car and breathed in the salt air of the North Sea, wondering how far down the water was. The view from the bluff was spectacular.

The sound of the big black sedan's engine seemed to have awakened the old building and her doors opened, spilling people onto the drive.

Kyle knew Matilda and Nikolai immediately.

Tor's mother was thin and fragile looking, but she wrapped Kyle in a tearful hug that was surprisingly strong. "I am so happy you both are finally here."

Kyle hugged her back. "As am I, Mamma Hansen."

Matilda loosened her hold and stepped back to look at Thor, who was walking shyly around the back of the car. She looked as shocked to see her grandson as Kyle had been to see Teigen.

"Oh my word. He really *is* the image of Tor at that age."

Kyle smiled at her mother-in-law. "I hope you have pictures. I'd love to see them."

Nikolai hefted one of the suitcases while Teigen claimed the other. "Welcome to Hansen Hall, Kyle and Thor. We've all been eagerly waiting for this day for a long time."

"Thank you, Pappa Hansen." She rested her hand on Thor's shoulder. "We're so happy to be here."

A petite woman with short, light brown hair and pale blue eyes stepped forward, smiling. She had a baby on her hip and a pretty little girl held onto her hand.

"Hello, Kyle. I'm Selby." She lifted the hand held captive by her daughter. "And this is Torhild."

Kyle squatted down to her niece's eye level the same way Teigen had to Thor. "I'm your Aunt Kyle. My son Thor is your cousin."

Torhild chewed a finger and looked at Thor who was now leaning against his mother.

"How old are you?" Kyle asked even though she knew the answer.

Torhild held up five fingers.

"Five years old? That's wonderful. Thor is five years old, too." Kyle put her arm around her son. "But he doesn't speak very much Norsk, so you'll have to teach him."

Kyle straightened and tucked her finger into the baby's hands. "This must be Jans. How old is he now?"

"Just turned four months. We waited to have him christened until his Aunt Kyle got here." Selby lifted her free shoulder. "We figured everyone would want to meet you, anyway."

Kyle looked around at the people gathered together: Nikolai and Matilda, Teigen and Selby, Torhild and Jans, and knew without any doubt that she and Thor were exactly where they should be.

Teigen and Nikolai carried her suitcases to the door while

Matilda linked her arm through Kyle's. "Let's get you both settled."

Kyle took Thor's hand and walked into Hansen Hall.

We're here, Tor. We finally made it.

※ ※ ※

Thor was itching to explore the fascinating old house and Selby assured her it was fine for him to do so, so Kyle placed him in Torhild's care.

"Remember that he doesn't know what he's allowed to do, so you have to show him," she said to her niece. "And come get me if he's naughty."

Torhild nodded solemnly.

Kyle looked at Thor. "Stay with Torhild, don't wander off on your own. And try to understand what she tells you. I'll be in our room unpacking or in the kitchen helping with supper."

Thor's eyes were bouncing everywhere but on hers. "Yes, Mamma."

"Okay, *dere to gå.*" Kyle said it in Norsk, knowing that it sounded enough like English for Thor to understand *you two go.*

It occurred to her that if she spoke Norsk to him while they were here and he was immersed in the language that Thor might learn to speak a substantial amount during the month they were spending in Arendal. When they got home she could easily build on that foundation.

"Thank you, Gjertrud." Selby handed Jans to a young red-haired woman before she followed Kyle into the room she would share with Thor.

"We do have domestic help here," she told Kyle as she opened the big pine wardrobe painted with traditional Nordic designs.

Selby turned to face Kyle again. "Mrs. Nilssen's the housekeeper and cook. Her husband was killed when the Germans attacked Norway ten years ago and she's been working for Matilda ever since. Gjertrud is her daughter—she's nineteen—and I employed her to help me with the children."

"This is a big house," Kyle observed as she opened one of

their suitcases. Her own little half of her duplex in Minneapolis could probably fit inside the great hall. "How long have you and Teigen lived here?"

"We moved in after the war ended, so Torhild was born here." Selby looked awkwardly apologetic. "We named her after Tor. Teigen insisted."

Kyle nodded. "He had every right to do that."

"We didn't know you yet. And with you being American..." Selby let the sentence fade away.

Kyle left her suitcase and approached Selby. "I know it was a shock to you all when you found out Tor was married, especially to an American you'd never heard of."

"It was. And just so you know, having Tor buried in Minnesota was very hard on Matilda and Nikolai."

Kyle swallowed. "I thought about having his body sent here, I really did. But then I realized that Thor would need a grave to visit so he'd know his father was a real person. And honestly I needed that, too. Our time together was so short. Does that make any sense?"

"It does." Selby took Kyle's hand. "I think you should tell them that. It might help them to hear things from your side."

"I will." Kyle squeezed Selby's hand. "Thank you. I hope I can count on your honesty all the time."

Selby smiled softly. "Even if it's hard?"

"Especially if it's hard." Kyle chuckled. "I haven't survived the last five-and-a-half years by running away from reality."

Selby's eyes narrowed. "I think you and I are going to need a night out together to compare our stories. It takes a strong woman to handle a Hansen man. I'd bet we're more alike than we know."

Kyle grinned. "I would love that."

She let go of Selby's hand and returned to her unpacking. "So tell me what to expect here. Like supper—does the whole family eat together? Do the children sit with the adults?"

"Normally Torhild has her supper in the kitchen because she's bored with us old people, but on special occasions she does join us." Selby winked. "You and Thor are a special occasion."

Kyle laughed. "So tonight we'll eat together, but Thor will

have his supper with Torhild in the kitchen as a rule. Got it."

"We'll have other guests this weekend as well." Selby hung up the blouse Kyle handed her. "Because the christening is on Sunday, our friend Dahl Holter, and Teigen's cousin Olina Bakke are coming down from Bergen. They'll be Jans' godparents."

Kyle handed Selby two more blouses. "They're coming together?"

"Yep. Because apparently they're *going* together." Selby looked at Kyle over her shoulder. "We introduced them a few months ago and I guess they're an item now."

"What does Dahl do?"

Kyle opened a drawer in the wardrobe and laid her lingerie inside, sad and worn cotton things that they were. What did a widow and single mother need expensive silk for? Better to be practical and spend her limited income on more important things.

"He's an actor."

Kyle's mouth fell open. "Really? Would I have heard of him?"

Selby shook her head. "I doubt it. He's a stage actor, so unless you attend theater in Oslo or Bergen you wouldn't have seen him."

Kyle put the last of her clothes in a drawer and closed the empty suitcase. "How did you get to know him?"

"He was my captain in Milorg—you know what that is?"

"Yes." Tor told her that Teigen became part of Milorg after being released from the labor camp. "So that's where you met?"

Selby nodded proudly. "I served for three years. I was a lieutenant. Teigen was a sergeant."

Kyle smiled at her sister-in-law. "I was a second lieutenant in the Women's Army Corps for a year-and-a-half. Until Thor happened along."

"I wasn't sure if the American Army allowed married women." Selby accepted the empty case and set it by the door.

Kyle hesitated, wondering if she should tell the truth. But someone was bound to figure it out.

If they haven't already.

"We weren't married until I found out I was pregnant. Even

though Tor *did* tell me he loved me and he asked me way before that." Kyle opened Thor's suitcase and handed Selby a pile of shirts. "Did anyone here compare the dates?"

"If they did, they didn't say anything." Selby put Thor's shirts in a drawer. "But now I have to ask you why you didn't say yes before the baby—is that the only reason you married Tor?"

"Yes and no." Kyle knew she had to tell Selby everything or nothing—there was no middle ground here. "I loved him so, *so* deeply. He was the most amazing man I ever knew. And I told him I loved him too, the first time he mentioned marriage."

Selby nodded, her brow furrowed. "So what held you back?"

"He was going away to war on another continent. I didn't think I'd ever see him again." Kyle heaved a weary sigh. "Turns out I was right."

"But you and he were…sharing a bed?"

"No!" Kyle wagged a negating finger. "We were only intimate one time, in a very weak moment. I was a virgin and I didn't think pregnancy could happen the first time."

"But it did." Selby watched her carefully.

"Thank God it did. Tor was so happy when I told him."

"He was?" Selby's expression eased. "That's good to know."

"He told me over and over that he was glad that he'd given me his child to remember him by in case anything happened to him." Kyle swallowed the lump that choked her. "Somehow I think he knew what was coming. But he trusted me to raise Thor and bring honor to his memory. I still thank God every day for that."

Selby wiped a tear. "So do we."

Kyle waved a hand around her. "And now He's given my son a fine, strong family to be a part of."

Selby came to Kyle and hugged her. "You're such a blessing to us."

Kyle couldn't speak past the lump anymore, but she held her petite sister-in-law close.

Thank you, Tor.

CHAPTER TWO

Teigen Hansen closed the door to his father's office and settled into one of the two chairs facing the desk. "Did you want to talk to me about Kyle?"

His father looked surprised. "No. But she seems lovely, don't you think?"

"I do. Selby's helping her unpack. We'll see what she thinks after that." Teigen gave his father a significant look. "My wife's a very good judge of character."

"Yes, she is…" Nikolai nodded distractedly. "Tell me, are you planning to teach in the fall?"

Teigen wondered if his father's mind was weakening. "Like I've been doing for the last four-and-a-half years? Yes. Of course." He paused. "I *am* the science department chairman, Pappa."

Nikolai steepled his fingers and stared at his son. "Why do you teach?"

This was another conversation they'd had—many times. "Because I have a family to provide for. And I enjoy it."

"Hansen Shipping makes enough to support you and them."

"I know that, Pappa." Teigen leaned forward. "But that's *your* livelihood. I don't expect to live a life of leisure at your expense."

Nikolai watched him carefully. "I'm going to retire."

The impact of those four unexpected words slammed into Teigen's chest. "You are? When?"

"When you and I decide what to do with the company."

Teigen and Selby had talked about this day and which path Teigen would eventually take, but he expected this conversation to be years in the future. And he still wasn't sure of his answer.

Over the centuries, the nature of their shipping business had changed with the times. The most significant change came in the last seventy years with the expansion of the rail system. Ten hours in a freight car going across Norway beat ten days at sea sailing around it.

"What are you thinking, Pappa?" Teigen asked.

"I only see two choices. I either sell the business or pass it to you."

Teigen pointed out the newly-arrived American glitch. "What about Tor's son? Doesn't he deserve some part?"

"He's too young to run it, obviously, and I doubt his mother has any interest." Nikolai sighed. "If we sell it, I'll split the money between you and the boy. You'll keep the Hall and all the land, of course."

That was fair. "And if I decide to run it?"

"I guess you should buy him out. Or maybe send profit checks every year. I don't know." Nikolai looked like he was carrying the weight of a glacier on his sloping shoulders. "I don't have the answer, Teig, and I never expected to face what we're facing."

None of us did.

"Is it my decision, then?" Teigen pressed. "Which route we choose depends on what I want to do?"

Nikolai nodded slowly, his gaze fixed on Teigen's. "That makes the most sense, doesn't it?"

Teigen was quiet for a minute. Then he asked the question that had to be asked.

"If I say sell it, will you be disappointed in me?"

Nikolai's brows plunged. "Is that your answer?"

Teigen put up his hands. "No, not yet! I have to talk to Selby before I decide anything. And I need to think about the two choices from all different angles."

His father looked confused. "Then why would you ask me such a question?"

"I need to know, Pappa." Teigen drew a bracing breath. "If I tell you to sell Hansen Shipping, am I betraying the family's legacy?"

Nikolai's expression shifted. "Five hundred years of Hansen trade ships? That is quite a legacy, no question about it."

"And if I end it—and I'm not saying I will—would that disappoint you?" Teigen's palms were sweating. "Would you be disappointed in *me?*"

Nikolai's eyes grew visibly wet. "After all you went through in the war and after losing Tor, you are the future of this family. Anything you decide will be fine with me, Teig. I don't have the strength left in me to fight any more battles."

"Oh, Pappa…" Teigen's voice choked.

Nikolai leaned forward. "I love you, son. And I'm damned proud of you. Nothing will ever change that."

Teigen nodded and cleared his tightened throat. "How soon do you want to know?"

"This month. Before Kyle and Thor leave."

Of course. "You want to tell them what Thor will inherit."

His father nodded again. "And I'd like to do it face to face in case she has questions."

Teigen rose to his feet and held out his hand. He was startled by how tired his father suddenly looked.

"Thank you, Pappa."

Nikolai gripped it and shook it. "No, thank you, son. I'll go along with anything you say."

ᚾ ᚾ ᚾ

Dahl Holter steered the car south in the town of Tvedestrand to start the last ten mile leg on the nine hour road journey from Bergen to Arendal.

"I'm glad I don't have to rush back to Bergen," he said as he rubbed his stiffening neck. "It'll be nice to spend time with

Teigen and Selby."

"Abandoning me is what you're doing," Olina grumbled. "I wish you'd come back to Bergen with me and save me from a lonely day on the train."

Dahl flashed a tired smile. "I'll be back before you have a chance to miss me."

She wrinkled her nose. "Just don't be sucked in by Selby's charms and forget all about me."

Dahl gave her another smile, this one strained by his annoyance. He regretted ever telling her that he fancied himself in love with Selby at one time and that Teigen swooped in and stole her out from under him.

Sort of.

Selby had actually never responded to Dahl's gentlemanly advances no matter how patient he was with her.

Teigen won her without even trying to.

At first Dahl was crushed, though he denied it and hid his feelings away—until they eventually withered and died from neglect. After that he was able to truly be friends with the couple. Now he would name them the best friends he had.

And that was why he was asked, and agreed, to be young Jans' godfather. It was a coincidence that Teigen's cousin Olina Bakke, who was tapped for godmother, lived in Bergen where Dahl was involved in the production of a play.

As director and second lead, he'd been there for the last three months. After closing this production last weekend, he was asked to take the cast and crew to Oslo with opening day in eight weeks.

Originally it was four weeks, but Dahl held out in the negotiations until he'd secured himself a much needed break.

Meanwhile, he'd spent time over the last few months with twenty-nine-year-old Olina, eight years his junior and very pretty, wondering if it was time for him to think about settling down.

If I ever want to be a father, I better get on it.

"So who's this other person who'll be there?" Olina asked, breaking into his thoughts.

"Tor's widow and her son," he reminded her.

"Oh, that's right. He married some American. Rather suddenly, if I remember correctly." Olina sighed. "Can't imagine what he was thinking."

Dahl had no answer for that. He'd met Tor briefly several years ago and couldn't say he knew the man at all.

Dahl drove in silence until he reached the turn toward Arendal. He drove down the hill into Arendal before turning right to drive up the bluff to where the ungainly Hansen Hall was perched.

"We made it!" he announced as he parked the car and climbed out. "And we have an hour to spare until supper."

Olina opened her door. "I wonder if I'll have time for a bath."

As Dahl unloaded their two suitcases from the trunk, the door opened and Teigen bounded down the steps. He clasped Dahl's hand and pulled him into a back-thumping hug.

"Good to see you, man!" he said.

"It's good to be here," Dahl responded. "Thanks for letting me stay a while. I need the break."

Teigen turned his attention to his cousin as he grabbed the handle of her suitcase. "Olina, how's life in Bergen?"

"More interesting now that I have such a handsome and charming escort," she teased and looped her arm through Dahl's. "This guy knows everybody!"

Dahl lifted his suitcase with his free arm and lowered his voice. "So? What do you think of the American so far?"

Teigen shrugged. "I haven't had much time to talk with her myself yet, but Selby absolutely loves her."

Dahl grunted. "That says a lot. In all the time I've known her, Selby's never had many female friends."

"Still doesn't. She's picky." Teigen grinned. "That's why she picked me."

Dahl was used to the ribbing by now and it no longer bothered him. "I'm picky, too. That's why I'm still single."

"Maybe not for long," Olina trilled.

"Oh?" Teigen looked surprised. "Is there news?"

"No, no, no," Dahl said quickly.

The last thing he wanted was for Olina to make premature

assumptions. He felt her stiffen beside him and knew he needed to soften his rapid reaction.

He turned and smiled into her irritated expression. "But we are going to be godparents together, so who knows where that might take us, eh?"

"Right." She was clearly trying to smile.

"Come on in, you two." Teigen walked to the door. "And meet the newest members of the family."

※ ※ ※

Kyle dressed in a light green blouse that brought out the green in her gray-green eyes and paired it with a conservative navy blue skirt. She didn't think wearing the slacks she'd adopted since being a WAC would be appropriate for her first supper with the Hansen family, especially with the addition of other guests.

She had her window open to catch the sea breeze and heard the car pull up. Car doors slammed as she brushed her shoulder-length hair and tied it out of her face with a silk scarf she'd had since she was in school—the first time. She added a light touch of lipstick and declared herself ready for whatever came her way.

Mentally as well.

"When's supper, Mamma?" Thor whined as he draped dramatically across his bed. "I'm hungry."

Kyle looked at her watch. Supper was still half an hour away. Making a nine hour time change in the last forty hours had messed up her system, so it was no wonder her son was grumpy.

Maybe Gjertrud will get him a snack.

"*Kommer*, Thor." Kyle held out her hand. "*La oss gå ned til kveldsmat.* Let's go down to supper."

At the bottom of the stairs Gjertrud took Thor's hand.

"Can you give him a little snack?" Kyle asked the girl. "He's really hungry."

"Of course." She smiled at Thor. "Torhild is having some lefse and butter in the kitchen. Let's go get you some."

Thor nodded, though there was no way he understood Gjertrud's words. But he understood her smile.

Kyle squared her shoulders, smoothed her hair, and walked toward the voices in the Great Hall.

It was still a shock to see Teigen; his resemblance to her memory of Tor was disturbing to put it mildly. At least this time the sight of him didn't make her cry.

Teigen was talking to another man who was slightly shorter than he and wore his sandy hair longer than her brother-in-law.

That must be the actor.

A quick glance around the room showed no sign of his Hansen cousin counterpart, just Matilda and Nikolai sitting on the sofa and sipping glasses of wine.

"Here she is." Teigen motioned Kyle forward. "Kyle, come meet our friend, Dahl Holter."

The actor spun slowly, a pleasant smile on his very handsome face.

That's him.

Tor's voice was so clear in her head that Kyle turned to look for him. Realizing she was being ridiculous, she quickly turned back to Dahl and flashed her best cover-up smile.

The smile faltered when she saw his bright blue eyes.

"Kyle?" Selby said. "Are you all right?"

Kyle made a dismissive sound. "It's the time change, I think. I didn't sleep much last night and I'm all upside down." She strode forward and held out her hand. "It's a pleasure to meet you, Dahl."

The actor was staring at her as if he wasn't sure what to think of her. He took hold of her hand but he didn't shake it, he just held it.

"It's a pleasure to meet you as well."

Kyle glanced at Selby to break away from a gaze that seemed to reach down inside her and jab at long-dead emotions.

Selby was frowning a little at Dahl. "Are *you* all right?"

"He's missing me of course!" a woman's voice chirped behind Kyle. The source of the voice brushed past her and stood on tiptoes to plant a loud kiss on Dahl's cheek. "Sorry I'm late. The bath was heavenly."

Dahl still held Kyle's hand and he hesitated before he let go. "This is Kyle Hansen, Olina."

⚔ ⚔ ⚔

Good God, man. Get a grip.

Dahl felt like someone had just put his life in a mixer, jumbled it all up, and dumped it back out onto the ancient stone floor of Hansen Hall. But he had no idea why.

Olina looped her arm through his in a common gesture that tonight inexplicably set his teeth on edge. "It's nice to meet you, Kyle. Welcome to Norway."

"Thank you." Kyle looked around. "Could I have something to drink?"

"I'll pour you a glass of wine," Teigen offered before Dahl could. "Is white okay?"

"Sure." Kyle turned back and gave Olina a faint polite smile.

Say something, you idiot.

Dahl cleared his throat. "I've been to America."

That clearly captured the beautiful widow's attention and her surprised eyes met his. "Oh? Where?"

"Iowa State University held a Nordic Theater Conference two years ago and I was asked to take part." It was still one of Dahl's prouder moments. "I directed a one-act play in Norsk."

Kyle looked sincerely interested. "Isn't that in Ames, Iowa?"

"It is. Where do you live?"

"Minneapolis. It's about two hundred miles north of Ames, so not too far considering the size of the country." She smiled shyly. "But I'm originally from a tiny town much farther north called Viking."

Teigen handed Kyle her wine and grinned crookedly. "Your town is named *Viking?*"

CHAPTER THREE

Kyle sipped the wine to give herself a moment to try and hold on to her once-again threatened composure.

"I know. It's a verb." She waved a hand in a casual gesture that belied her quivering core. "Tor teased me mercilessly about it."

"That sounds like my brother." Teigen looked at Olina. "Would you also like a glass of wine?"

"Yes, please." She nudged Dahl with her elbow. "I thought Dahl would ask me."

"What?" The actor's face flushed. "Oh, sorry."

Kyle wanted to take her mind off Tor before her exhaustion caused her to start blubbering at the mention of his name. "Selby told me you're a stage actor."

Dahl nodded. "Guilty as charged."

"Ooh!" Olina interrupted. "I just realized you both have men's names!"

Selby looked at Kyle and, if she read the other woman's expression correctly, then Selby was just as jarred by Olina's non sequitur as she was.

"Yes we do," Kyle said, facing Olina again. "But my name is actually a combination of my parents' names, Kylli and Ole."

Olina blinked. "Oh! The KY and the LE. How clever."

"My mother simply loved the meaning of my name," Selby offered. "It comes from combining the old Norse words *selja* and *by* which means *willow by a farm*. She didn't think that was too masculine for a girl."

"I love your name," Kyle said honestly.

Selby smiled. "And I love yours."

"Olina means light."

Kyle looked at the pretty blonde. "That's… nice."

Selby's responding cough sounded more like a laugh. Kyle slid her glance to Selby but her sister-in-law was looking the other way.

Kyle turned back to Dahl, who was standing still like an uncomfortable statue. "Tell me more about your acting. I'm fascinated."

"Well… I have a theater degree from the University of Oslo, which was called the Royal Frederick University when I attended sixteen years ago," he began. "I'd been acting and working backstage…"

He flashed a charmingly crooked grin. "Anything to get experience, you know?—for five years when the Germans attacked us. Then I joined the resistance."

"And he started the Royal Shakespearean Acting Troupe as a cover for our activities," Selby injected. "We passed information and supplies up and down the coast while we traveled from town to town to perform."

Kyle was impressed. "That's brilliant."

Selby smiled up at her tall husband. "That's where Dahl and I met Teigen."

"Tor told me about that." Her heart clenched a little less this time when she said his name. "I'd love to hear—"

"Looks like it's time to eat," Olina interrupted. She pulled Dahl toward the door. "Ready?"

ⵎ ⵎ ⵎ

Dahl sat next to Olina and across the table from Kyle and Tor's son Thor, which suited him fine. The American was interesting and she asked interesting questions, which he loved answering when Olina didn't interrupt.

"Your Norwegian is very good," he complimented at one point.

"Thank you. That's what Tor said, too." She shrugged shyly. "My grandparents moved to Minnesota from Solbergelva. They took Solberg as their surname because it was easier for Americans to say and spell than Schjelderup."

"So you grew up speaking both Norsk and English?"

"I did."

When Thor's head bobbed forward, Kyle excused herself to take the boy to bed.

"Do you need help getting him upstairs?" Dahl asked.

Kyle looked at him like she didn't understand why he'd ask her that. "No. Thank you, though."

Once she and Thor were gone, Olina kicked his foot under the table. "What was that about?"

Dahl stared at her. "What? Offering to help her?"

"Yes. You obviously offended her." Olina's lips pressed together in disapproval.

Did I?

He didn't think so. But he'd make a point of asking her tomorrow just to be sure, and apologize if he'd violated some American bit of etiquette that he wasn't aware of.

The last thing he wanted to do was upset Kyle further.

As an actor he was keenly aware of facial expressions, always noticing the subtleties that would make the difference between a good performance and a great one. Judging by what he saw, tonight had been very difficult for the young widow.

Dahl looked at Teigen. He remembered how much Tor and Teigen looked alike and was sure that his resemblance to her dead husband was a large part of her discomfort.

That would be disconcerting for anyone.

Dahl thought there was more going on behind those guarded gray-green eyes than only that, but he would rather ask her outright than guess wrongly. He didn't know why it mattered to him so much, other than he didn't want to be the cause of any more pain in her life.

ᚾ ᚾ ᚾ

Kyle donned her cotton bathrobe and tiptoed out of her room. Thor slept soundly, but she hadn't been able to fall asleep even though she was completely done in. She thought maybe a bite of something to eat or maybe another glass of wine might push her tired body into falling asleep when it was still broad daylight in Minnesota.

A small fire spilled a faint light into the hallway outside the Great Hall. Teigen explained that the old stone structure tended to be chilly even in summer, so a small fire was nearly always burning there. As she passed the door she saw Teigen's long frame draped in a chair. Her brother-in-law held a glass in one hand and stared into the fire.

Kyle didn't want to disturb him, but her slippers made a noise and he turned to look at her.

"Kyle? Did you need something?"

She walked forward. "I'm having trouble falling asleep. I was thinking another glass of wine might help."

Teigen set his glass on the floor and motioned her forward. "I'll get it. Come sit."

Kyle sat in the chair that was at a right angle to Teigen's. "Are you usually up late?"

"No." He poured her wine. "I just have some things on my mind."

She watched his face in the dim light as he carried the glass to her and reclaimed his seat. "I hope I haven't done anything to concern you."

Teigen's brow twitched. "Not at all."

"But my being here has made everyone think of Tor, hasn't it?" She rubbed her fingertips against the cool wineglass. "I know I've been thinking about him a lot more now that I'm here."

"That's not your fault." Teigen lifted his glass from the stone floor. "And I know when you look at me, you see him."

Kyle nodded a little. "But the more I talk to you, the more I see the differences."

"We are actually very different," he said before lifting his glass to his lips.

Kyle took a drink of the buttery white wine. She wanted to tell Teigen what Tor had said about him and now seemed to be the perefect time for it.

"Tor told me about the last time you were together," she began. "I think you need to hear what he said about you."

Teigen snorted. "You mean when I told him his shoes were hard to fill?"

Kyle's voice was soft, but it seemed to fill the hall. "He said you have no idea how hard he ran to stay ahead of you."

Teigen's head turned toward hers. "What?"

"He said you were school smart. You went to the university and got a degree in chemistry and became an upper-level school teacher." Kyle smiled a little at the memory. "He really respected you a lot."

Teigen was clearly shocked. "He never told me that."

"He said all he ever did was train his way into an Olympics that never happened."

"But by doing that he achieved something that very few people could!" Teigen was obviously trying to process what she was telling him. "And then he joined the Norwegian Army and went off to teach soldiers in America."

"Think about it, Teigen," Kyle said gently. "The reason Tor joined the Norwegian Army as soon as Norway was invaded was because every one of his competitive opportunities disappeared that same day."

"He could have done other things," Teigen objected.

Kyle shook her head. "I think it was the only path he believed was open to him at the time."

Teigen downed the drink in his glass and got up to refill it. "I never thought of it that way. I thought he was just being impulsive. Maybe even selfish."

Kyle sighed. "I can understand that. But I can also tell you that he had absolutely no idea what he was going to do once the war was over."

Teigen reclaimed his chair. "He didn't want to come back here? Take over Hansen Shipping?"

"I'm sorry to say it, but no." Kyle tried to discern whether

Teigen was offended by that, but she couldn't tell. "He knew he wasn't cut out for it, you know?"

"Yes. I do know." Teigen took a gulp of his fresh drink.

Before Kyle could think about what that statement might mean Teigen asked, "Was he a good leader?"

"Pardon my language, brother-in-law, but he was a *damn* good leader and his men respected and loved him." Kyle shifted in her seat. "Not only that, but there were dozens of world-class competitive skiers who joined the Tenth Mountain Division to train the soldiers, and they knew and respected Tor as well."

Teigen quirked a smile. "He was always the popular one."

Then he looked horrified, like he'd let something slip that he shouldn't have. "I don't mean—"

Kyle put up a hand to stop him. "I spent a year at his side, Teigen. I know *exactly* what you mean."

He looked contrite. "I guess you would."

"I also know what was truth and what were assumptions. Your brother wasn't nearly as much of a ladies' man as the ladies hoped." Kyle chuckled a little. "He even kissed me in public once just to get the other WACs off his trail."

Teigen wagged a finger at her. "I doubt that was the only reason, considering how things turned out."

"Maybe not," Kyle conceded. She took a drink to hide her warming face behind her wine glass.

"Selby told me about how Thor came to be."

"Oh, no." Kyle slapped her forehead.

"Don't worry about it. I don't."

Kyle considered her brother-in-law in the firelight. "I loved Tor with all my heart. You need to believe that."

"I do," he said in a sincere tone. "Why else would you have cried when you first saw me?"

Kyle stared into her wine glass watching the reflection of the flames shimmer through the golden liquid. "I wouldn't be who I am today if I hadn't met your brother. And as painful as it's been without him, I wouldn't change a minute of it."

Teigen was quiet for a while and they sat in companionable silence with only the occasional pop of the fire making any sound.

"Will you marry again?" His murmured question sounded overly loud though he was hardly more than whispering.

Maybe.

"Tor told me to in his survivor's letter. He told me to find a father for Thor."

Teigen looked sideways at her. "Are you seeing anyone?"

Kyle huffed. "I'm a single mother who completed her bachelor's degree in psychology in less than four years and is halfway through her master's degree. I haven't had time to date."

"Do you want to marry again?" he pressed.

Kyle stared into the fire and considered the question.

She'd been so busy for the last five years she hadn't had time to think about it. But with Thor starting school in a couple months, and expecting to finish her dissertation by Christmas, a lot of lonely free time was suddenly looming in front of her.

It would be nice to have a man in her house, she thought. And in her bed. And to start working on those siblings for Thor.

Could she fall in love again?

"I don't want to live my life alone," she admitted. "But God's going to have to drop him right in my path, because I have absolutely *no* idea where to find him on my own."

Teigen leaned over and held out his glass. He had the oddest look on his face.

"Here's to finding love," he said.

"Again," she clarified.

Kyle tapped her wine glass against his tumbler and then downed the remainder of its contents.

CHAPTER FOUR

July 6, 1950

The next four days passed in a blur of adjustment. Having the sun set at eleven-thirty at night only to rise again four hours later was complicating Kyle's distance-disrupted sleep patterns. Twice she apologetically succumbed to the need for an afternoon nap.

Kyle tried to make up for her fog by helping in the kitchen when Mrs. Nilssen would let her, though her knowledge of Norwegian cooking was clearly Americanized.

She also strove to keep a watchful eye on Thor and make sure he wasn't getting on her hosts' nerves. Thankfully he got along well with Torhild and followed her everywhere, indoors and out.

And during those first four days Kyle learned three things. The first was that Olina didn't like her.

Kyle had only one explanation for the younger woman's attitude, and that was the six-foot-three, sandy-haired actor with eyes as bright a blue as Tor's had been. Dahl was a lead theater actor in part because he was gorgeous, that much was obvious.

She's afraid Dahl will like me.

The concept surprised her. She'd never been the one others

were envious of. At least she'd never been aware of it.

Olina seemed to think she'd hit the jackpot by being paired with Dahl as Jans Hansen's godparents. She claimed the man every time Kyle approached by grabbing his hand or his arm or tucking her shoulder under his. Olina's sights were set on nabbing the actor, and Kyle believed he knew it.

The second thing she learned was that the more Olina leaned in, the more Dahl was pulling away. If he'd been initially interested in Teigen's cousin, that interest was clearly fading in the klieg light of Olina's possessiveness.

Kyle hadn't said or done anything that Olina could say was remotely flirtatious or derisive. The same could not be said for her.

"Did I offend you at supper last night?" Dahl asked when she emerged from her first night in Hansen Hall.

Kyle was surprised by the question. "When?"

"When I asked if you needed help getting Thor to bed." He looked adorably contrite. "Olina said that I did, and I wanted to assure you I didn't mean to be rude."

Rude?

What game was she playing?

Kyle shook her head. "No. That was very kind of you. Why would she say—" Then she remembered her reaction to his offer and her cheeks flamed. "Oh! I was the rude one, I'm afraid. I'm so sorry."

Dahl seemed confused by that, so Kyle hurried to explain. "Thor is five years old and I've been both mother and father to him ever since he was born. Your offer took me by surprise, is all."

Dahl rubbed his chin, his fingers smoothing his short beard. "Of course you have. I should have known you could do it alone."

"And I should have accepted the help," she countered.

"Let's make an agreement." Dahl stuck out his hand and grinned. "If I offend you, you'll tell me."

"Only if you'll do the same." Kyle smiled into his eyes and shook his hand. His large, warm, and strong hand.

Stop it.

The third thing she learned was that Matilda Hansen really was as frail as she looked.

"When I met her during the war, after Teigen and I were married, she was suffering from lack of adequate nutrition," Selby told her. "He spent three days building a pig pen deep in the woods under an outcropping of rock. And he hid a chicken coop inside the chapel."

Kyle felt punched by her relatively easy war experience. Tor tried to tell her it was true, and now she was hearing it first hand. "Because the Nazis took everything?"

Selby nodded. "They were truly horrible men."

"How did you survive?"

"When Dahl started the acting troupe, he had the blessing of the Germans because he was promising *cultured* entertainment for their officers." She wrinkled her nose. "And when that traitor Quisling stepped up a year later, he jumped on board as well."

Kyle hated that she was so ignorant about what happened here. "And that meant what, exactly?"

"That meant we stayed in hotels that catered to the Germans, so there was always enough food and heat, and the accommodations were very comfortable." Selby looked a little guilty. "The townspeople weren't always sure what to think about us. Especially—well, never mind. Have you seen the photographs yet?"

That shift piqued Kyle's interest. There was some kind of story there.

Later.

"The family photographs? No. But I'm dying to."

Half an hour later, Kyle was sitting next to Matilda on the sofa in a room lined with tall bookcases. From what Kyle could tell, they were mostly filled with ancient books.

Selby sat on Matilda's other side. "Wait until you see these. The resemblance is amazing."

Matilda opened the thick leather-wrapped cover of the square album. She pointed to the sepia-colored photo mounted on the first black cardboard page.

"These are my parents, Alfhild and Sigurd Bakke. Olina's grandparents. This was taken on their wedding day."

Kyle looked at the young woman with loose waist length hair streaming from under a huge crown-like headdress. The breast piece on Alfhild's vest was richly embroidered and Kyle could only guess at the colors.

"She looks so young," Kyle said.

"She was eighteen." Matilda sighed. "This was taken nearly seventy years ago."

Matilda turned the thick page. "These are Nikolai's parents. It was taken about the same time."

Another earnest young couple stared, unsmiling, from the old brown photograph in an elaborate pressed matte.

Kyle smiled at her mother-in-law. "I can see the resemblance between Nikolai and his father."

Matilda nodded. "The family has very strong genes."

She turned another page. "This is our wedding portrait from nineteen eleven."

The sepia tone remained the same, but Matilda wore a gown that was contemporary for the age. "I wore my bunad at the wedding, but I was a modern girl and wanted to be photographed in a modern gown."

She chuckled sadly. "I wish I had a photograph of that instead. You girls would be amazed at my bridal crown. It was huge. I was marrying a Hansen, after all."

Selby and Kyle's gazes met over Matilda's head and smiled. They both knew what marrying a Hansen was like.

"And here are the boys."

The faces of Tor and Teigen, taken in nineteen-nineteen when the brothers were six and four, were not only similar to each other, but Kyle could have inserted a snapshot of Thor in his father's place and no one would be the wiser.

"Oh my Lord," she breathed. "I can't believe it…"

Matilda touched the photo reverently. "What a pair they were."

Selby looked at Kyle again. "He is the image of his father, isn't he?"

Kyle nodded. "Do you have any more?"

Matilda turned the page. "Here they are in upper-school. I believe that was Tor's final year, so nineteen-thirty-one."

Kyle stared at her husband in the shiny black-and-white modern photo. She saw the man he was becoming so clearly that it actually hurt her chest.

"He had so much ahead of him then, didn't he?"

Matilda wiped a tear and turned the page. Stuffed between the pages were a dozen yellowing newspaper clippings. "This is when he was competing."

Kyle lifted the articles and scanned them. "Could I have one of them?" she asked. "For Thor?"

"Take several," Matilda answered. "He needs to know his father."

Kyle laid her hand over Matilda's thin bony one. "Thank you so much."

"Thank you, Kyle. If it wasn't for you and Thor, we wouldn't have anything of him left."

◢ ◢ ◢

Olina was gone.

The collected Hansens waved at the departing car as Dahl drove her to the train station. Teigen looked down at Selby, wondering if she was thinking what he was. But the christening was yesterday, the deed was done. It was too late to change anything.

"I know what you're thinking," Selby said as she led him away from the house. "It should have been Kyle, not Olina."

How did she know?

"I do like Kyle." He glanced back to make sure they were out of earshot. "And I don't remember Olina being such a pill."

"I don't either," Selby admitted. "But she's twenty-nine now. The war interrupted her courting years and then handed her a much smaller platter of choices."

Teigen grinned. "Very poetically put."

Selby elbowed him. "I'm serious. I think she's getting desperate."

"And that's why she was so annoying whenever Kyle was around?" he suggested. "Olina saw her as competition?"

Selby laughed. "There's no competition."

Teigen found that comment disappointing. "So you think Dahl's happy with Olina?"

"Good God, no!" Selby stopped walking and faced him. "Watch. He'll be sniffing around Kyle as long as he's here. In fact, I predict it starts as soon as he gets back."

"Dahl and Kyle." Teigen nodded thoughtfully. "I was wondering if it was my imagination. Or maybe just wishful thinking."

Selby tilted her head and smiled impishly. "Wishful thinking, eh?"

Teigen shrugged. "We'll have to wait and see of course, but if they do connect then we're assured she won't marry an American and fade away from us."

Selby's expression softened. "Keeping her and Thor close, means keeping Tor close."

Teigen ran a knuckle down his wife's cheek. "Is that silly?"

"No. Not at all." She grabbed his hand and squeezed it. "It makes perfect sense."

Teigen started walking again, still holding Selby's hand. "If the two of them do hit it off, and she'll have him, it will make my own decision so much easier."

She looked up at him. "How?"

Teigen heaved a heavy sigh. "I love teaching."

"I know. And you're very good at it."

Teigen kept walking while he ordered his thoughts.

"I trust Dahl. I trust his character," he finally said.

"He's a good man, there's no question there," Selby confirmed. "And he's been a very good friend to both of us for many years."

"If Kyle married Dahl..." Teigen ran his free hand through his hair. "I could tell Pappa to sell the business without worrying that someone would take advantage of Thor's inheritance."

Selby stopped walking again. "Is that the deciding factor?"

"It's a large part of it, to be honest," Teigen admitted. "I hate the idea of an American getting his hand on Thor's money when we can't do anything about it."

"Kyle wouldn't let that happen," Selby declared. "She's far too smart for that."

"But what if something happened to her?" Teigen pressed. "Say she got hit by a bus or something before Thor turned twenty-one. Then her husband would have control."

"What a terrible thought!" Selby scolded.

"It could happen, and you know it," Teigen argued. "And we *are* talking about a lot of money. Enough to take him through college and buy a house free and clear."

"And if Kyle invests it wisely, it could double in sixteen years." Selby sighed. "I see your point."

"So we're agreed?" Teigen asked hopefully.

"Agreed that we want Kyle to marry Dahl? Sure."

Teigen laughed. "Not just that. Agreed to do what we can to help them along."

Selby's jaw dropped. "Are you serious?"

"Why not? It could be fun."

She pointed a finger at him. "But we can't be obvious about it or it'll backfire for sure."

ᚾ ᚾ ᚾ

Kyle heard the commotion in the entry hall and hurried to see what was happening. It had to be more than just Dahl returning from the train station—there were too many voices.

When she rounded the corner, Dahl was standing inside the door with a lanky young man with short blond hair and soulful brown eyes who was grinning from ear to ear. "Hey everybody! Look what I found at the train station!"

Teigen rushed forward and wrapped the boy in a suffocating bear hug. "Ben! We didn't know you were coming back!"

When he let go, Selby grabbed Ben in a hug of her own which ended in a loud kiss on his cheek. "I'm so glad to see you!"

Ben's gaze moved around the group and landed blankly on Kyle. "Uh, hello."

Teigen motioned her to his side. "Ben this is our sister-in-law from America, Kyle Hansen."

Understanding washed over the young man's face. "Oh! You're Tor's wife."

"Yes. I was," Kyle forced herself to say calmly. "And our son Thor is running around somewhere with Torhild."

"The cousins are getting along wonderfully, even though Thor doesn't have any Norsk yet," Selby added.

"And this," Teigen said proudly to Kyle. "Is Benjamin Thorkelsen Isaksen, our foster son."

Foster son?

Isaksen is a Jewish name.

"Teigen found me hiding in the woods after the Nazis killed my mother and took my father and brother. He kept me safe until the war ended." Ben had obviously recited that explanation many, many times before. He held out a hand. "It's nice to meet you."

Kyle smiled at the engaging young man and shook his hand. "It's nice to meet you, too, Ben."

"Ben's an artist about to start his last year of university. And we *thought* he was in Italy for the summer." Teigen shot Ben an inquisitive look. "What's going on?"

"I saw what I needed to see. Florence was incredible, but Rome was old, hot, and stinking." He shrugged. "So I decided to head home."

"Well, I'm very glad to see you," Selby smiled happily. "I'll tell Mrs. Nilssen to set another place at supper."

ᛚ ᛚ ᛚ

Because of Ben's surprising appearance, Thor and Torhild were again having dinner in the dining room with the adults. The addition of Ben to the group as a replacement for Olina was like pouring sunshine into a fog.

Ben's stories about his month-long journey through Italy were both hilarious and awe-inspiring.

As the main dish was served and conversation slowed, Thor turned to Kyle. "He's funny."

Kyle nodded. "Yes he is. Can you understand him?"

"No, but he makes funny faces. I like him better than Olina." Thor paused. "Mamma, do you like Olina?"

Kyle glanced apologetically around the supper table before

she smiled at her son and answered him in English. "Not in the least bit. She was very annoying. But she's gone and I don't think she's coming back."

Thor's gaze bounced to the subject of his next question and then returned to Kyle. "Do you like Dahl?"

Kyle forced herself not to look at the actor. "Yes I do. I like him very much. Do you?"

Thor's mouth twisted. "I guess. But you like me best, right?"

Kyle hesitated; that question signaled trouble ahead.

Now is not the time.

"Of course." She ruffled Thor's hair and faced a table full of inquisitive adults. "He was just asking why Olina left and Dahl's still here," she said in Norsk.

Everyone nodded and went back to their meal. Everyone except Dahl, that was. He was looking at her pensively.

When Kyle lifted her brows in question, he just smiled and stabbed his fork into his red deer steak.

CHAPTER FIVE

July 9, 1950

When Dahl drove away from the Arendal train station three days ago he felt like he'd unloaded a huge burden. If he was unsure before, he was certain now. He needed to break from Olina.

Dahl understood that the post-war marriage situation for women in his country—in all of Europe for that matter—provided vastly diminished opportunities. And he also understood that he was considered prime marriage material because of his relatively young age and his leading-man appearance.

If he doubted it, all he had to do was step outside the stage door after any play that he had a part in. Ninety percent of the crowd waiting there was comprised of women looking for him, all asking for autographs and pictures. He could have his pick of them and he knew it. If he was the type of man that played with women, he'd never have to spend another night alone.

Throughout the war Dahl spent most of his time unsuccessfully wooing Selby, and then dealing with the rejection of her sudden marriage to Teigen towards the end. After the Royal Shakespearean Acting Troupe was forced to disband, he moved to Bergen and continued his work in Milorg until the Germans surrendered.

After the Nazis were arrested and Norway's occupation ended, Dahl was able to help Norway rebuild her theater tradition. In the process he transitioned from always playing the handsome but often uninteresting leading man to directing and taking on more meaty roles.

Of course, that decision meant not having a permanent home. Dahl traveled between Bergen and Oslo two or three times a year, so he rented rooms near the theaters and lived his life out of trunks.

Dahl was very satisfied with his career and his income—with his Spartan lifestyle he'd managed to put away quite a lot of money, especially in the last three years. And he had good friends in the theater community in both cities so he was never lacking companionship.

But at thirty-seven years of age he *was* lacking a wife.

And children.

And a house to put them in that was his.

Why that was weighing on his mind so heavily these last two weeks was a mystery. Maybe because of this trip to Arendal with Olina and her obvious hope that being godparents to little Jans would prompt Dahl to make a commitment to her as well.

Olina was a truly lovely woman; there was nothing overtly wrong with her. She just didn't prompt any sort of physical response in Dahl when he saw her—no stepped-up heartbeat, no unquenchable smile, nothing like that. Nor did he miss her when he was away from her.

He grinned crookedly into the mirror while he shaved.

Now I know how Selby felt about me.

Dahl resolved to phone Olina that same evening and let her down gently. Sadly, he doubted he'd miss her.

Kyle, however, was a completely different story.

From the minute he laid eyes on her he was gobsmacked. Nearly speechless. He thought for a moment that someone was pushing him toward her, though that had to be his imagination.

Now that Olina was gone, Dahl and Kyle made a neat and comfortable foursome with Teigen and Selby. After the children were put to bed, they spent the last two evenings in a variety of cozy activities that Teigen or Selby suggested.

Tonight they were going to walk around Arendal's charming center and enjoy the summer's long twilight. Teigen mentioned a tavern on the pier that had tables outside and suggested they might have a drink there after the walking tour.

Dahl smiled without meaning to.

He stared at himself in the mirror, razor poised for the last stroke, and wondered if his life was about to change.

N N N

Kyle felt like the last three days in Arendal were redefining her entire life and she felt completely knocked off balance by the realization.

Dahl was the culprit.

The handsome, charming, kind, and unexpectedly humble culprit.

The culprit who stirred something in Kyle that she hadn't felt since she met Tor.

That was six years ago.

Kyle knew Tor wanted her to remarry, and she had every intention of doing so once she finished her master's degree. Of course, that's what she said about finishing her bachelor's degree. And now the suggestion by her professors that she continue on and get her doctorate in psychology loomed.

How long could she put this off? She was already thirty-one and Thor was growing up fast. Seeing him here in Arendal had shown her aspects of his upbringing that now worried her.

The first was his possessiveness of her. Of course that made sense. Since he was born he'd never had to share her time or her affections with anyone else. And those siblings Tor urged her to give him were nowhere in sight.

Kyle always blamed her busy schedule and her son's needs for refusing the invitations that occasionally came her way.

But a shocking realization hit her these last days and she was struggling to accept it. She hadn't been putting Thor first out of selfless devotion. She did it out of fear.

And that fear was centered in Tor.

Kyle knew she was making her husband into some sort of ideal man and the love they shared almost holy. But Tor had flaws that she refused to think about. And their love was perfect because it was brief.

They never had the chance to actually live in their marriage. To experience the struggles inherent in any relationship and work through them. To resolutely love each other more deeply as they grew old together.

Kyle held the lipstick tube in midair and her gaze dropped from the mirror to the sink.

If she married again, she would have the chance at that sort of life-long relationship—and deep down she was afraid that her love affair and marriage with Thor's father would seem lacking by comparison.

And it should.

Kyle dropped the lipstick and grabbed the sink for support as that staggering concept surged through her mind.

That was why she was afraid. Because she knew that a fifty-year marriage would be far more intimate and satisfying than one that ended after three months.

Tor knew that. And he wanted that for her if he died.

Kyle sat on the edge of the porcelain tub. Her hands were shaking and her pulse thrummed in her ears. She'd failed Tor. She hadn't done what he wanted her to do.

I've been selfish.

The bathroom seemed to grow brighter. The tears Kyle expected didn't materialize. She felt the last remaining wisp of her grief-induced fog blow away.

It's time.

Kyle stood. She looked at herself in the mirror, surprised at what she saw.

She was smiling.

ᚾ ᚾ ᚾ

Kyle's new resolve was tested within minutes.

"I want you to stay home," Thor grumbled. "And read me

stories."

Kyle sat on Thor's bed. "I'll read you one book, but then I have to go."

"Why?"

Kyle picked a short fairytale from Thor's little stack of picture books. "Because your aunt and uncle want to go out and show Dahl and me around Arendal."

Thor frowned his deepest frown. "I don't like him anymore."

Kyle opened the book. "Who? Dahl?"

Thor nodded vehemently and crossed his arms. "He told me to stop running."

"Where were you running?" Kyle looked into Thor's eyes. "Was it in the house again?"

"Torhild runs in the house."

"And did Dahl tell her to stop, too?"

Thor clearly saw that he was losing ground and he switched tactics. "Dahl's not my Pappa. He can't tell me what to do."

"Dahl's an adult who is staying in this house just like we are," Kyle countered. "And if you are doing something you're not supposed to, then he *can* tell you to stop."

Thor's eyes welled with tears. "That's not fair!"

"I'm afraid it's completely fair." Kyle gave Thor a sympathetic smile. "But don't worry. When you're a grown-up, you can do the same thing."

That apparently wasn't helpful.

Thor's mouth turned down at the corners and his lower lip trembled. "You like him better than me."

"No, sweetheart. I like him *different* than you. You are my best little boy and I will always love you. Nothing will ever change that." Kyle kissed him soundly on the forehead and laid the book in his lap. "We've used up our time and I have to go. But you can stay up and look at your books until I get home."

Thor pushed the book off the edge of the bed.

Kyle's second concern about Thor's upbringing which had recently come to light was being played out in front of her, and she sadly realized it was also her fault.

My son is spoiled.

She tried so hard to make up for Thor not having a father at home that she gave her son whatever he wanted whenever it was possible for her to do so. But if she was going to marry someone and have more children, that needed to stop.

Not to mention that when he went to kindergarten in the fall he would need to know how to play nicely with the other children there. He couldn't always have things his way.

Kyle stood up and told herself that she knew psychology and this was the right thing to do.

"You don't have to look at your books if you don't want to," she said sweetly. "I'll be home before it's dark."

And then she picked up the light sweater that was lying across her bed and walked to the bedroom door. She blew Thor a kiss and left the room, closing the door behind her.

ᚾ ᚾ ᚾ

"It was so hard." Kyle looked miserable. "But I didn't realize how I was spoiling Thor until I've seen him here. I thought I was doing a good job and raising a good boy."

Dahl took her hand and squeezed it as they followed Teigen, Selby, and Ben down the hill into town. "You *have* done a good job, Kyle. And he *is* a good boy."

Kyle sighed. "Being away from home like this, I can see some things he needs to learn that I haven't taught him."

"He's only five," Dahl reminded her. "There's time."

She looked up at him, her expression sheepish. "Thank you for scolding him when he was running in the house."

Dahl smiled. "Don't worry. I scolded Torhild, too."

Dahl didn't let go of Kyle's hand when she stopped talking. And she didn't pull hers away.

Until Teigen turned around to say something to them. Did she think he would disapprove?

Would he?

Dahl decided to talk to Teigen later and make sure his friend didn't object to Dahl courting his brother's widow.

Dahl stopped like he walked into an invisible wall.

I'm going to court Kyle?

Kyle halted one step farther and turned back to look at him.

"Is something wrong?"

Dahl drew a deep breath. "I—um—no."

He forced an awkward smile and started walking again, allowing the gap between them and the trio walking ahead of them to grow. "Can I ask you something personal?"

Kyle's glance slid to the side and then met his again. "Sure."

"Do you think you'll you marry again?"

N N N

Now Kyle stopped walking. Was Dahl reading her mind?

That's him, Kyle.

Kyle spun in a circle looking for the source of her dead husband's voice. Of course, he wasn't there any more than he was the first time she heard him.

"Kyle?" Dahl looked appropriately worried.

She rested one hand on her hip and the other against her forehead. "What?"

"Did I offend you by asking you that?" He spread his hands in supplication. "I didn't mean any disrespect. Please believe me."

"No. I'm not offended." She drew a shaky breath. "I—have been thinking about that a lot. Lately."

Dahl looked at her oddly. "Lately?"

"Since coming to Arendal." Kyle shook out both of her hands and started walking again.

Dahl fell in step beside her. "Have you come to a decision?"

She nodded without looking at him.

"What have you decided?"

"I think it's time I started... I mean, I don't know how, but... Thor does need a father," she babbled. "And brothers or sisters."

"So if I understand the language of Kyle," Dahl teased. "You do want to remarry, because it's good for Thor—"

"—and me." she interrupted him to be sure he didn't get the wrong idea. "I don't want to live alone for the next fifty years."

She risked facing him. "I do want to find love again."

Dahl nodded slowly. "I understand."

He reached for her hand and wrapped it in his. When he did, she heard Tor's voice again.

That's him, Kyle.

ᚾ ᚾ ᚾ

Selby elbowed Teigen. "Did you hear that?"

Teigen grinned. "I certainly did."

"You need to tell Dahl that he has your blessing to court Kyle," Selby whispered. "So he doesn't waste the time she has here by being afraid he'll make you mad if he does."

Teigen wanted to look back at the other couple but didn't dare. "Do you think he could win her in three weeks?"

Selby laughed. "Have you taken a good look at him?"

Teigen snorted. "Men are more than their looks."

"And you know Dahl as well as I do." Selby bumped her shoulder against Teigen's arm to punctuate the point. "He's a wonderful man inside as well as out."

They were almost to the Arendal town square, so Teigen turned around and walked backward. He flashed a broad grin when he saw the other couple walking hand-in-hand.

And this time Kyle didn't pull her hand away from Dahl's.

"Come on, you two!" He laughed, delighted by the sight. "I've worked up a thirst."

Dahl grinned back. "Don't rush us. We'll catch up."

Teigen laughed again and turned back around.

We're counting on it.

CHAPTER SIX

July 10, 1950

"You are asking for my permission to court Kyle?" Teigen asked Dahl when the men were hunting rabbit the next day. Mrs. Nilsson had a favorite stew recipe that she wanted to make and Teigen assured her that he and Dahl would supply the meat.

Dahl nodded nervously. "I thought I should, since she's your brother's widow."

Teigen lifted the shotgun to his shoulder and squeezed the trigger. The rabbit leapt in the air before collapsing on the ground. Teigen jogged forward to collect it as he thought about what he wanted to say.

He was tying the rabbit's leg to his line when Dahl reached him. He looked at his friend, deciding to ask the hard questions now rather than when it might be too late.

"I know this sounds like a stupid question, but if you court her, what do want to happen?"

Dahl hesitated, looking at Teigen crookedly. "I think I want to marry her."

"You've only known her a week," Teigen challenged. "How can that be possible?"

"I honestly don't know." Dahl looked confused. "Maybe it

was seeing her with Olina."

"Olina?" Teigen liked his cousin, but Dahl had a point. The two women were very different. "How?"

"Don't get me wrong, your cousin is a lovely woman. She'll make the right man very happy. She's just not right for *me*." Dahl shrugged. "Like I wasn't right for Selby."

Well said. "Go on."

"Kyle is a special kind of woman. And I can understand why Tor married her before he shipped out." Dahl smiled. "When you meet someone who seems so perfect, you don't waste time."

"She was pregnant," Teigen reminded him.

"He would have married her anyway."

Teigen's brows pulled together. "How do you know that?"

Dahl threw up his hands. "I don't know. But I do."

Teigen looked at his friend carefully. "What's going on with you?"

Dahl's shoulders slumped. "You're going to think I'm crazy."

"Try me."

Dahl rested his shotgun his shoulder. "Ever since I first saw her, I felt like I was being pushed toward her."

"Pushed?" Teigen repeated. "By what?"

"A hand that wasn't there." He considered Teigen with narrowed eyes. "Are you happy now? I said it."

Teigen started walking again. He knew Dahl was a level-headed guy. He was the ranking officer in their Milorg group and his decisions were always solid ones. The man wasn't crazy, no matter how this all sounded.

And Teigen also knew his brother. If anyone could reach past the barrier to the afterlife, Tor would be the one to do it. That's the sort of man he'd always been.

Was that possible?

"So you're serious about this?" Teigen said to Dahl once his friend was walking beside him again. "You want to court her with the hope of marrying her?"

"I do. Unless there's something that I discover about her in the meantime that turns me away." Dahl looked like he couldn't believe his own words. "But only if you agree, Teig."

"I'll tell you what, Dahl. I couldn't be happier if this works out," he said. "Not only for you, but for me."

"For you?" Dahl stopped walking. "What do you mean?"

Teigen faced his friend. "I'm going to tell you something in strict confidence. At least for now."

Dahl's expression showed his concern. "Understood."

"I think I'm going to sell Hansen Shipping."

Dahl stepped back, his eyes wide. "Really?"

Teigen nodded. "My father told me last week that he wants to retire."

Dahl looked askance at him. "And you don't want to take it over? Why not?"

Teigen shrugged. "I don't want to stop teaching."

"Does Nikolai know that?"

"He does."

Dahl tilted his head. "So how does my courting Kyle have anything to do with that?"

"Because Thor will receive Tor's portion of the sale." Teigen watched as understanding washed over Dahl's face. "And if you're married to Thor's mother, then I know his money will be well managed and not end up in some American's pocket."

"That does make sense…" The wheels in Dahl's head were obviously turning. "Kyle will still want to live in America…"

"That's where their life is, isn't it?" Teigen stated. "Are you willing to move to Minnesota?"

Dahl's brow furrowed. "I might be."

"You better decide that before you court her. Or at the least, talk about it with her," Teigen warned. "I could be wrong—she might move to Norway. But I highly doubt it."

N N N

Kyle stood in the doorway watching Thor and Torhild playing in the courtyard with their new toy cars. Thor was making typical rumbling engine noises when Dahl and Teigen walked through, carrying three dead rabbits on the line.

Thor's eyes widened. He abandoned the cars and ran to the men. He looked equally fascinated and horrified.

"Did you shoot those?"

Kyle answered the question instead of translating it. "They went hunting for our supper, Thor."

Teigen handed Kyle the rabbits. "Will you give these to Mrs. Nilsson? We'll go wash up."

"Sure." Kyle accepted the bounty and headed toward the kitchen.

Thor was behind her in a flash. "Why'd they shoot the bunnies?"

Kyle looked down at her city-born, city-raised son and realized he had no idea where meat came from. For a farm girl from Viking, that was an embarrassment.

"Mrs. Nilsson is going to butcher them and make stew."

Thor frowned. "What's butcher?"

"Take off the fur and cut up the meat," she eased into the explanation.

"Can I watch?"

Kyle hesitated, wondering if that was a good idea. On the farm, killing and butchering the animals that they raised or hunted was a common occurrence, one that she'd experienced her whole life. But for Thor, the new experience might prove too gruesome.

She decided to leave the decision up to Mrs. Nilsson and hope for the best.

"He'll get in my way," she grumbled. "Maybe another time."

Kyle was surprised at her own disappointment, but she understood the housekeeper's point.

"She says you can't stay and watch this time. Maybe when she makes chicken." Kyle figured the plucked bird would look less like a furry little pet and its disembowelment would be easier for Thor to accept.

He frowned. "Does she take the feathers off and cut up the meat on a chicken? Is that where chicken comes from?"

"Yes." *I am a complete failure*. "Now go back outside and play with Torhild. It's a beautiful day."

"What about fish?" Thor asked as he trudged toward the back door. "Does she take off the skin and cut up the meat, too?"

"Yes." Now was not the time to quibble about what marine

flesh was actually called.

When he reached the door, Thor turned around and looked at her. "Can I go hunting?"

N N N

Dahl stepped up behind Kyle and smiled at Thor. "*Skal du ha det gøy?*" Are you having fun?

Kyle's stomach fluttered a little at the sound of his voice. That was interesting. Pleasantly so.

"He wants to know if he can go hunting," she told Dahl in Norsk.

"Yes. Of course he can go hunting!" Dahl's smile widened. "Teigen has a pellet gun he can use."

"Stop talking like that!" Thor shouted in English.

Kyle looked at her son in surprise. "Like what?"

"Like *sel hanska poe vee yah*," he imitated the sound and cadence of Norsk. "I don't like that."

"That's Norwegian, Thor, you know that. It's the language the people here speak," Kyle chastised.

Thor pointed at Dahl. "I don't want you to talk to him like that."

"To Dahl?" Kyle glanced at him and looked back at her son. "Why not?"

"Because I don't want him to like you."

Kyle was staggered by her son's jealousy. "But I like him, Thor. In fact, I like him very, *very* much. And I want him to like me back."

Thor scowled. "I don't."

"Well he just offered to take you hunting!" she blurted. "Should I tell him no?"

Thor's eyes rounded with disbelief and he looked from her to Dahl and back again while Kyle wished she could suck those words right back out of the air. Thor with a gun? The idea terrified her, even if it was only a pellet gun.

Dahl laid his hand against the small of her back. "I'll make sure the boy is safe, Kyle."

Even though Dahl's assumption of her objections was spot

on, Kyle wasn't ready to give in just yet. "He's too young."

Dahl's voice was calm. "I was shooting a real gun by the time I was five. So was Tor, I'll bet."

"Don't bring him into this."

"Don't coddle him, Kyle," Dahl countered. "Isn't that what you were saying last night?"

"When you have children of your own, you can tell me how to raise mine!" she snapped.

"*Stop talking like that!*" Thor stamped his foot and looked like he was about to cry. "I want to go hunting!"

Kyle was caught in a steel trap between the two of them. If she dug her heels in, she would lose both Dahl's and Thor's respect. But to give in…

She whirled on Dahl and jabbed his chest with a stiff finger. "If anything happens to him, I *will* kill you. I was in the Army. I know how."

Dahl saluted her. "Yes ma'am."

"Don't mock me!"

"I'm not. But I was a captain and I do outrank you."

Kyle huffed and faced her son. "I'll let you go hunting with Dahl if you'll stop shouting at me about him."

Thor looked at the Norseman standing by her side. He was clearly torn between his desire to shoot at something and his dislike of her growing friendship with the man.

"When you can agree to that, we'll talk about when you can go. Understood?"

Thor turned around and stomped back to Torhild who sat on the ground surrounded by their toy cars and staring at him like he was the oddest thing she had ever seen.

ᚾ ᚾ ᚾ

Dahl waited until after their rabbit stew supper, when Thor was in bed and Kyle's mood was soothed with a glass of wine, before he asked her to take a walk with him. He wanted to have a serious discussion with her and he wanted to do it in private, away from Teigen, Selby, and the inquisitive Ben.

They took the path away from town and along the bluff.

Dahl brought a blanket for them to sit on and enjoy the beautiful view of the North Sea.

He began the conversation with, "I'm sorry if I sounded harsh today. Thor is your son and you should raise him as you see fit."

Kyle looked contrite. "And I didn't mean to snap at you. You made a good point."

"That's done, then." He stopped at a grassy spot and spread the blanket on the ground, smiling. "May all our arguments end so simply."

Kyle laughed at that. "Amen."

The couple settled on the blanket. The sky above was still blue, but the eastern edge was beginning to darken to purple as the sun lowered in its long elliptical arc.

"Tell me about your life in America," Dahl prompted. What's it like?"

Kyle raised her brows and drew a deep breath. "Well, I own a Victorian duplex in Minneapolis. I live in half and I rent out the other half to pay the mortgage. And I go to school at the university."

As he asked more questions and Kyle talked, Dahl put together a pretty complete picture of what life in America would entail. Though Kyle had been a working mother all this time, he wondered if she would be willing to stop and raise their children if he married her. At least until the children were in school.

He decided to ask.

"That's an interesting question," she admitted. "As a counselor I could work part time and hold sessions in my home, I suppose…"

"I could go along with that," Dahl said without thinking.

Kyle looked at him sharply. "What would you do?"

"I'd look for work in the theater, I think—I'd teach acting or maybe produce or direct for an established company." He shrugged. "Iowa State University talked about offering me a position, but I wasn't interested at the time. I could write to them and see if that's still a possibility."

"That's two hundred miles south of Minneapolis."

He narrowed his eyes as he considered the situation.

"Couldn't you work on your thesis at home and drive up once a week to meet with your professors?"

Kyle nodded slowly. "I'd have to ask, of course. But something like that might work out."

Dahl stared at her, stunned by their conversation. "Kyle…"

She gasped and her hand flew to her mouth. Her gray-green eyes widened and her expression was somber when her hand fell back to her lap.

"What are we doing?"

"I think…" He paused, honing his thoughts. "We're both wondering if we could make a future work between us."

Kyle brushed her breeze-blown blonde hair out of her eyes. "You mean before we jump in and get our hearts ripped out?"

Dahl nodded. "Is that what it feels like to you?"

"Yes. It does, actually."

"So what now?" His smile grew slowly. "May I court you?"

She looked cautiously optimistic. "What will Teigen think?"

"I already asked him."

"You did?" she yelped. "What'd he say?"

"He was thrilled," Dahl said honestly. "So what do *you* say?"

Kyle's expression shifted. "I say you should kiss me."

Dahl didn't need to be asked again. He slid one hand around Kyle's neck and buried his fingers in her hair. He pulled her close, his eyes pinned to hers until hers closed.

When their lips touched it felt like being struck by lightning. Electricity fizzed through his veins and every nerve in his body tingled. If Dahl had any doubt about their connection, it dissipated in that instant.

"Did you feel that?" he whispered when their long and deep kiss ended.

Kyle looked like her world was as shaken as his. "Yes. But you better kiss me again to be sure."

CHAPTER SEVEN

July 13, 1950

For the last three days Kyle had felt like a young girl again, giddy and full of hope. When Dahl's lips met hers the first time, she couldn't help but think of Tor—Dahl's was her first romantic kiss in five-and-a-half years.

But it took less than thirty seconds for her to realize that Dahl was a completely different man with a distinct appeal that was all his own. And she was smitten.

To the core.

She convinced Dahl to keep his physical displays of affection limited to times when Thor either wasn't in sight or after he went to bed.

"It's not only my feelings that we have to consider," she reminded Dahl. "I can't ignore his—and right now with being so far from home his world is out of kilter."

"Of course." Dahl brushed her hair out of her eyes and kissed her forehead. "Are you ready to let me take him hunting? That might be a good start."

Kyle drew a deep breath and held it. She knew what the answer should be, but she was reluctant to loosen her hold on her son. He was Tor's only legacy and he still seemed so young.

But Thor had said he was sorry about yelling at her, and he hadn't griped about her conversing with Dahl since. And honestly, the two of them were conversing much more frequently since their first kiss.

The first of many.

"Breathe, Kyle," Dahl chided. "It'll be fine. I promise you."

She released her held breath. "Okay. You can take him."

Dahl grinned. "I'll get Ben to come along. Thor likes *him*."

Kyle's fingers twisted into a nervous knot. "When will you go?"

"There's no time like the present." Dahl planted a solid kiss on her lips. "And it's a beautiful day."

And that was that.

Thor looked like an extra Christmas was happening when she told him. He squealed and jumped up and down, doing a little dance in the room before Kyle had him change clothes.

"Do what Dahl shows you to do," Kyle instructed. "If you misbehave, even the littlest bit, you won't be able to go *ever* again. Do you understand?"

Thor's head bounced in an enthusiastic nod. "Yes, Mamma."

Selby stood next to her as they watched Dahl and Ben, with Thor between them, walk out of the courtyard and head toward the forest.

"He'll be fine, you know," Selby assured her. "Dahl knows how to handle a gun and he'll show Thor the right way."

"I know." Kyle looked at her sister-in-law. "But it's so hard to let go."

Selby sighed. "We all have to. That's turning out to be the hardest part of being a mother, in my opinion."

"Agreed." Kyle faced Selby. "Let's go bake something. A reward for the mighty hunters on their triumphant return."

ᚿ ᚿ ᚿ

The trio appeared two hours later, Thor proudly carrying his pellet gun like it was the mightiest of machine guns. He ran up to her, grinning like a hyena.

"I hit the tree, Mamma!"

"Did you?" Kyle wasn't sure what she expected, but thought that was good news.

"He did well." Dahl took the gun from Thor. "He learned how to load the pellets and shoot the gun. But we only shot at trees today."

Ben smiled. "Those two shot at trees. I managed to take out a couple of crows."

Thor tugged on her sweater. "I want to go again, Mamma. Can I?"

Kyle looked at Dahl, who was obviously glad that Thor didn't hate him at the moment. "Would you take him again?"

"Happily."

Ben handed Dahl his shotgun. "Without me, I'm afraid. I'm heading back the university tomorrow. I'm taking the bus to Oslo in the morning."

Kyle smiled at the young man. "Thank you for spending time with Thor. He's going to miss you."

Ben ruffled Thor's hair. "He's a good kid."

Kyle considered her filthy son; sweaty dirt smudged his cheeks and bits of leaves stuck in his hair. "I think we'll do your bath before supper today. And Aunt Selby and I made almond cookies for dessert."

"Yay!" Thor squiggled in an outburst of joy. "Can I have one now?"

"If you wash your hands first."

When Thor bolted toward the bathroom, Kyle looked at Dahl, her heart full of gratitude. "Thank you."

Dahl smiled at her, his blue eyes glowing. "Thank you for letting him go with me."

She was beginning to believe the voice.

This very well might be him.

July 15, 1950

Dahl was walking toward the front door when he heard giggling and the scrape of furniture coming from the Great Hall. He turned to look through the doorway then sprinted inside to catch Thor in mid-tumble.

The five-year-old was apparently trying to reach a sword that was mounted on the wall. To reach his goal, he'd lifted a wooden chair on top of a side table and was climbing the wobbly tower when Dahl spotted him.

"You know you're not supposed to do that!" Dahl shouted at Thor then turned to Torhild. "Why didn't you come get someone?"

Torhild's lips trembled. "I told him not to."

Dahl set Thor on his feet. "That was very dangerous, Thor! You could have gotten hurt!"

Thor stared up at him, looking exactly like a puppy caught chewing a slipper.

Until his mother appeared.

Kyle looked at Dahl, the wooden chair which had clattered to the floor, and her son. "What's going on?"

"Thor tried to use that chair on top of that table." Dahl pointed at the evidence as he spoke. "To try and reach that sword."

Kyle's expression darkened and she strode straight toward Thor. "Are you all right?"

The boy shifted from puppy to bulldog. "He can't yell at me! He's not my pappa!"

Kyle looked at Dahl. "You yelled at him?"

"After I caught him in mid-air? Yes I did," Dahl huffed. He wasn't the guilty party here.

"I hate you!" Thor bellowed at Dahl. Then he ran from the room.

Kyle started to follow him but Dahl grabbed her arm. "He nearly went head-first onto the stone, Kyle. He would have suffered a bad concussion—or worse."

She glared up at him. "I need to go to him."

"What he did was dangerous. He has to understand that."

Kyle gave a quick shake of her head. "That's my job, not yours. Just because we're dating doesn't give you the right to discipline my son."

"If this becomes more than dating, it'll be my job too," Dahl reminded her before he let go of her arm. "Go on then. Do what you need to do."

She hesitated. "Thank you."

Then she ran after Thor.

※ ※ ※

Kyle knew Dahl was right. Thor was wrong. But how was she going to bring peace between the two of them? If she didn't figure that out, she'd be returning to Minneapolis as unattached as when she left.

Thor needed to be dealt with first. "You know what you did was wrong, don't you?"

Thor didn't answer—a sure admission of guilt. Instead, he repeated his previous stance, "Dahl can't yell at me."

"We've talked about this, Thor. Any adult in this house has the right to stop you when you do something wrong." Kyle grabbed his arm to assure he was listening. "And if Dahl hadn't been there, you would have been badly hurt."

"He's not my pappa."

Thor's litany pushed Kyle to the edge of her patience. "No, Thor. He's not. Your pappa died in Italy fighting the Nazis. Right?"

Thor looked shocked at her harsh tone. He nodded a little.

"Someday, I'm going to get married again," Kyle said sternly. "And when I do, you will have a *different* pappa."

He frowned. "What?"

"My husband will live in our house, sleep in my room, and be the pappa of our family." Kyle's head of steam took over and she charged through her terse explanation. "When that happens, I will have more babies. And you will have brothers and sisters. You won't be the only child anymore."

Thor stared at her like she had just given him the worst news he could imagine. "Who are you getting married with?"

"I don't know for sure." She paused, wondering if she dared to tell him the truth. Might as well prepare the way now, not later. "But it could be Dahl."

※ ※ ※

Dahl waited in the Hall wondering just how angry Kyle was with him, because he was damn angry with her.

Was he crazy to continue to pursue her? Thor was always going to be a reminder of her first husband and the boy wasn't going to be pleased with any man who wanted to share his mother's attention.

He better be sure she was worth the struggle before he spent one more hour with her.

Dahl walked to the sideboard and poured himself a glass of aquavit. Then he poured a glass of wine.

As he did, Kyle walked up next to him. "Is that for me?"

Dahl handed her the glass. He wasn't smiling.

"So... how angry are you?" she ventured.

"Very."

Dahl walked to an upholstered chair and dropped into it. He sipped his drink before he looked at her.

Kyle followed and sat in the chair next to his but she wasn't looking at him. "I don't blame you. I didn't handle any of that well."

"Nope."

Kyle nervously twirled her glass. "I'm sorry, Dahl. I should have fallen down and kissed your feet, not taken you to task for saving my wayward son."

"Yep."

She finally looked at him then. "Will you accept my apology?"

He sipped his aquavit again before he answered. "I will. But I have to ask you something."

Kyle gave a little nod. "You want to know if I have room for a husband in my life."

How did she know?

Dahl watched her carefully. "What's your answer?"

Her eyes welled and she ineffectually blinked the tears back. "It's not going to be easy, I know that. But it's what I want."

"Are you sure, Kyle?" he pressed. "Without any doubt?"

"I am, Dahl." She wiped her cheek. "Will you be patient with me?"

"We only have three weeks before you fly back to

Minneapolis," he pointed out. "Call me crazy, Kyle, but in my opinion you either go back as a married woman, or a completely unattached one."

Her eyes rounded. "Is this a proposal?"

"Not yet." He dipped his head to the side. "But it has the possibility of turning into one, I think."

"You're crazy," she murmured.

One corner of his mouth lifted. "Are you as crazy as I am?"

"You're sweeping me off my feet," she admitted. "That worries me."

"We're not children, Kyle. We just need to decide to make a commitment and then work together to keep it."

Kyle set her glass on the low table in front of them and wove her fingers together before she faced him again. "What about love?"

Dahl sighed. "Can I say I love you? Not yet. But my feelings for you are growing faster than I thought possible."

"Mine too," she whispered without the trace of a smile.

That's encouraging. "If things between us continue as they have been, then in a few weeks I'd be marrying a woman who completely owned my heart."

"And moving to America?"

"And moving to America," he promised.

Her gaze dropped and lifted again. "Are you ready to be a father to a spoiled five-year-old?"

Dahl leaned forward and pinned her gaze with his. "That little guy needs me, Kyle. Maybe even more than you do."

Kyle stared at him. "Are you real?"

He chuckled and stuck out an arm. "You tell me."

Kyle grabbed his arm and squeezed it. "Seems solid."

"Good." Dahl withdrew his arm. "Now you need to promise me something."

"What?"

"You have to trust me."

She frowned. "Trust you with what?"

"With Thor. You need to let me treat him like my son while you're here. He and I need to figure that out together."

"I don't know…" Kyle retrieved her wine glass from the

table in front of her and finally took a drink. "What if it doesn't work out?"

"It's better that we find that out now," he said kindly. "Before licenses and ceremonies and airplane tickets are involved."

Kyle was clearly struggling with his suggestion. "I don't want him to end up hating you."

"He loved me the day I took him shooting, remember?" Dahl smiled. "I want more time with him doing things like that."

Dahl could see Kyle's resolve setting in. He could already read her moods better than any woman he'd known—even Selby.

She heaved a sigh. "You're right. I'll trust you with Thor."

"Good." He set his glass down and stood. Grinning at her, he held out his hand. "Now kiss me to seal the agreement."

Kyle took his hand and he lifted her from her chair. He wrapped his arms around her in a tight hug.

"I *am* falling in love with you," he whispered. Then his lips sought hers.

Kyle's response was warm and eager—so eager, in fact, he wondered if she'd been holding back before. He was submerged in her touch, lost in her kiss, aware of nothing but the woman snuggled in his arms.

"*Nooo!*"

Thor's anguished scream shattered his blissful world.

CHAPTER EIGHT

Dahl let go of Kyle and whirled around to face an enraged Thor. But he wasn't looking at Dahl. He was glaring at his mother with all the fury a five-year-old could muster.

"I don't like that!" he shrieked.

Then he bolted down the hall toward the back of the house.

Kyle started to go after him.

"Kyle!" Dahl barked.

She turned to look back at him, her pupils wide enough to steal the color from her eyes and the effects of their passionate kiss blurring her lips. "What?"

"Give him a minute, okay?" Dahl said. "He's angry at you this time, not me."

"No. He's angry at both of us," she said sadly.

Teigen ran into the room. "What happened?"

Selby rounded the corner right after him. Her eyes swept the room. "Is everyone okay?"

"Yes." Dahl wondered if Kyle would tell them or if he should. It was probably her place since it was her son who exploded. "Kyle?"

Her cheeks bloomed red. "We were kissing. Thor saw us. He's… not happy."

Teigen and Selby exchanged looks that seemed odd for the situation.

"Kissing?" Teigen asked, his eyes twinkling. "What's going on between you two?"

Selby smacked his chest with the back of her hand. "As if you don't know."

"I don't know details." Teigen rubbed the spot but he was smiling. "Will you tell us?"

Again Dahl wondered which one of them should speak. He decided to start with, "I asked Kyle if she would let me court her."

Kyle was clearly distracted by Thor's outburst, but she pulled her attention back to Dahl. "We've been talking about our future. If there could be one."

"And now we've hit this bump." Dahl closed the space between him and Kyle.

He smiled into her worried eyes. "Let me talk to him, Kyle. He needs to hear *me* say that I'm not going to take his mamma away from him."

She looked at him like he was simple. "How do you plan to do that? He doesn't understand Norsk, Dahl."

"No, but I speak English," he said realizing with a shock that he'd never mentioned that. "I'm out of practice, true, but I can converse with a child well enough."

ᚾ ᚾ ᚾ

Kyle froze in disbelief.

Her pulse surged in her ears. This couldn't be happening again! Another Norwegian suitor hiding the fact he spoke her language?

Why is this always happening to me?

"You. Speak. English," she growled.

Dahl's expression and tone were cautious. "Yes…"

Her brow lowered and she glared at him. "Since when?"

"Since I was a theater major. English was required as a second language." He cleared his throat nervously. "Probably because of Shakespeare. Or Oscar Wilde. Maybe Eugene

O'Neill."

"Why didn't you *tell* me?" she cried.

Dahl looked confused now. "I wasn't intentionally keeping it a secret. Your Norsk is so good, much better than my English, that I never thought to talk to you in English."

Kyle put a hand over her brow and wracked her memory. What incriminating things had she said in front of Dahl when she thought he couldn't understand her?

Only that she didn't like Olina.

And that she did like him.

She felt her cheeks grow tight with embarrassment.

Another thought occurred. "Did you speak English to Thor when you went shooting?"

"Of course." He shrugged. "How else could I teach him what to do?"

I should have figured that out.

"Damn it." Kyle walked in a circle, staring at the stone floor with her hands on her hips.

"Kyle?" Selby approached her. "What's wrong?"

Kyle looked at her sister-in-law. "Nothing. Really."

"You're not acting like it's nothing," Selby challenged. "What's going on?"

Kyle looked from Selby to Teigen. His face displayed the same concerned confusion as Dahl's and Selby's. Of course it did. None of them knew about Tor's intentional deception. She hadn't planned to tell them about it, but it seemed that now she'd have to.

"When Tor first came to Camp Hale he was assigned a translator," she began. "That was me. It's why I enlisted and it's how we met."

"But Tor spent a lot of time in England." Teigen looked to Selby and Dahl for confirmation. "Did he really need a translator?"

"As it turns out, no. But I didn't find that out until… for months."

Kyle decided they didn't need to know exactly *how* she found out and she didn't look at Dahl as she continued.

"In the meantime, we'd fallen in love and he asked me to

teach him English."

"Oh, dear." Selby laid a hand on Kyle's arm. "You must have felt so betrayed when you found out he was lying to you."

God bless you, Selby.

Kyle nodded.

"Did he tell you why he kept that secret? He must have had a good reason." Teigen was clearly hoping his brother could be vindicated.

Kyle hated to say more about Tor in front of Dahl, but if he was going to be her next husband he needed to hear it all.

"Tor said he was very attracted to me and he didn't want me to be reassigned. He wanted me to stay with him."

Teigen grunted. "That's Tor."

She risked a glance at Dahl. His expression was somber but he didn't seem upset by her words, so she kept going.

"He also said he thought it might be useful if others thought they could talk openly in front of him. He might learn secrets."

"Did that happen?" Teigen asked.

Kyle huffed a laugh. "Only when he overheard the prisoners of war speaking German, which he spoke fluently. But he told me about that."

Dahl took Kyle's hand and turned her to face him. "I am so sorry, Kyle. I had no idea."

Kyle gazed up into Dahl's bright blue eyes and her distress seemed to drown in their beautiful pools. "No, you couldn't have."

He laid a hand over his heart. "I promise that I have no more secret skills." His eyes twinkled a little. "Do you?"

Kyle chuckled. "Only my ability to ruin any recipe."

"I guess it's a good thing I can cook, then." Dahl kissed the back of her hand. "Let's go find Thor. He should be calmer by now."

N N N

The problem was, they couldn't find Thor.

Kyle, Dahl, Teigen, and Selby combed the rambling house from top to bottom without luck. Even Torhild didn't know where he was.

"Maybe he went outside," Dahl suggested.

"Could he have gone into the woods?" Kyle was terrified by that suggestion. "Followed your path from when you went shooting?"

"He might have, I suppose." Dahl was halfway to the back door. "Teig? Any other ideas?"

"A couple. I'll come with you."

The two men jogged out the back door.

Kyle looked at Selby. "Tell me I don't have anything to worry about."

"I don't think you do. He's probably sitting under a tree somewhere throwing rocks at birds."

Kyle didn't know what to do with her hands. "Maybe we should talk to Torhild again? See if she has any ideas?"

***

"Thor!" Teigen shouted.

"Thor! Where are you?" Dahl shouted.

"Maybe you shouldn't call out," Teigen suggested. "If he's still more angry than scared, he might not answer you."

Dahl thought about the look on the boy's face before he ran away. As much as he hated it, he admitted, "You're probably right."

"Thor!" Teigen bellowed. "It's Uncle Teigen. Where are you?"

A moment later, he shot Dahl an apologetic look and added, "I'm alone now! Where are you?"

The men stopped walking and listened. Birds flitted through the trees, chirping and squawking. Squirrels scolded them. The pine trees whooshed in the breeze.

But no little boy's answering call joined them.

"Let's check where Ben and I built a secret pig pen during the war," Teigen suggested. "It's protected by an outcropping of rock, so he might have crawled in there."

"Good idea," Dahl said softly, just in case.

He followed Teigen to the spot and was impressed by how

hidden it was.

"We transplanted these pine saplings to camouflage it." Teigen looked up at the trees that were now taller than he was. "Obviously they survived."

Dahl pushed his way past the trees and squatted under the overhang. The pinecone-strewn ground there was soft, its surface disturbed only by pine cones and fox tracks.

"There's no sign of anyone being here," he called back to Teigen.

Damn.

Dahl clambered back out. "Any other ideas?"

Teigen nodded. "One just came to me, but I'm not sure he'd know it existed."

"It's worth a shot though, right?"

"Sure." Teigen turned back toward the house. "It's in the stable."

Dahl matched his friend's long strides. "Did you have a safe place hidden in the stable?"

"Yep." Teigen gave Dahl a doubtful look. "But the hay bales are stacked in front of the door. Thor would have to know it was behind there and then pulled the bales out of the way."

"Does Torhild know it's there?"

Teigen blew a disgusted sigh. "She certainly does."

The men started to run.

ᚾ ᚾ ᚾ

The stack of bales was diminished by use and would not be restocked until the end of summer. And several were lying on the ground in disarray.

"He couldn't lift them, but it looks like he could push them," Teigen whispered. "Can you see the door?"

Dahl nodded. He motioned for Teigen to stay put and tiptoed to the nearly-hidden opening. He stood still and listened for a minute. Something was definitely shuffling inside.

I hope it's human.

And five.

The space between the bales and the slightly ajar door was

narrow and dusty. Dahl knew he wouldn't be able to squeeze inside without being heard. At least he'd be blocking the only exit so Thor couldn't get away.

He backed away, a sudden inspiration hitting him.

"I'll be right back. Stand guard," he told Teigen.

Dahl hurried out of the stable and gathered up a handful of pebbles. He put them in his pocket, then went back inside.

"I'm going in. If I don't come right back out, then he's fine and we'll be talking."

Teigen gave him a thumbs-up.

Dahl went to the back of the stable again, said a quick prayer, and wedged his way through the door.

Light seeped into the space through a slit under the eaves that would be undetectable from the outside of the building. In the dim light he saw Thor curled in the corner.

"Go away!" he grumbled. "Leave me alone."

Dahl stepped closer and sat on the wood-plank floor next to the boy. "You can stay in here if you want. But your mamma's very worried about you right now."

Thor looked at Dahl like that unsettling possibility had never occurred to him, but he said nothing.

"I'm glad I found you, though," Dahl said. "I wanted to have a man-to-man talk with you. Is that all right?"

Thor shrugged. "About what?"

"About your mother."

"You leave my mamma alone."

Dahl nodded like he understood. "Do you love your mother?"

"Yes."

Dahl reached into his pocket and pulled out a pebble. "Hold this. It means you love your mother. Does she love you?"

He scowled. "Yes."

Dahl set a pebble on the ground. "That means she loves you. Did she love your father?"

He shrugged again.

"I'm going to guess that she did." Dahl set a second pebble on the ground. "Do I need to take away the one that means she loves you, now?"

Thor scowled. "No."

"That's the right answer, Thor. Well done. Now," Dahl pulled the rest of the little rocks out of his pocket. "Do you have a dog?"

The question clearly piqued his curiosity. "No. But my grandma does. She has two dogs and a cat."

"Do you love the dogs?"

He nodded. "But not the cat. She lives in the barn and hisses at me."

"Fair enough." Dahl handed him two more pebbles. "Do I need to take away the pebble that means you love your mother?"

"No…"

"Another right answer. Who else do you love?"

Thor named his grandmother, grandfather, and Torhild. Dahl gave him three more rocks. The boy needed two hands to hold them all.

Dahl held out his palm with two pebbles in it. "If these are my pebbles, who do you think I love?"

Thor stared at Dahl's hand.

"My mamma?"

"That's one. Who's the other?"

Thor stared into Dahl's eyes. "Me?"

Chapter Nine

Tears streamed unheeded down Kyle's cheeks as she stood by the secret door and listened to Dahl tenderly explain how love worked to her son. She didn't think her heart could stand being so full.

Teigen had burst into the house a few minutes ago and shouted, "We found him! He's fine!"

Then he grabbed Kyle's hand. "Follow me and be quiet!"

He pulled her into the stables and pointed to the space between the hay bales and crooked door.

"Stand there and listen," he whispered.

"That's right," Dahl said. "The second pebble would be you, but only if you agree to that."

Thor was quiet.

"Now here comes the most important part, Thor. Are you listening?"

Thor's response was barely audible. "Yes."

"A person like you, me, or your mamma can collect as many pebbles as they want, one for everyone they love, right?"

"Right," Thor whispered.

"How many do we have to give away?"

"None?"

"That's right, Thor. None."

Kyle heard the muted clink of the little rocks hitting each other. "We add love when we love new people. We never take love away from someone else."

The voices paused for a moment.

Kyle almost called out when Dahl spoke again. "Your mother will never stop loving you, even if she starts loving me. Do you understand that?"

"I think so…"

"And if you let me love her, then I'll love you, too."

Thor must have been thinking about that because he didn't respond immediately. "I guess."

There was a rustle of movement.

"So, do you want to go shooting again tomorrow?"

Thor's voice was completely different now. "Can we?"

"You bet. Right after breakfast."

"Can I shoot a rabbit this time?"

Dahl chuckled. "You can certainly try, son. Are you ready to go see your mamma now?"

More movement and the scrape of shoes on wood. Kyle slid out of the narrow space and stood on the other side of the hay bales with Teigen, wiping her cheeks on her sleeve.

Dahl emerged first. He held Thor's hand as the boy followed him. When Thor saw Kyle, he ran into her arms.

ᚾ ᚾ ᚾ

Dahl watched Thor hug Kyle while Kyle smiled at him over her son's head. Her eyes glittered with unshed tears as she beamed at him and Dahl thought no woman on earth could ever look so beautiful.

Thank you, she mouthed.

Dahl laid a hand over his heart and dipped his chin.

He was all in now and there was no going back. If he wasn't sure before today, his talk with Thor made it clear.

I love you, he mouthed to Kyle.

Her smiled widened impossibly and the tears spilled down her cheeks. *I love you too.*

He chuckled, wondering who else in the world experienced their first declaration of shared love so silently. No matter, he'd make sure he said it out loud at the first opportunity.

Selby appeared in the stable door. "Teigen? Doctor Gustavsen is here."

"Coming," Teigen said as he strode from the stable.

"What's going on?" Dahl asked Kyle.

"Matilda isn't doing well, I'm afraid." She let go of Thor and tousled his already messy hair. "Why don't you go find Torhild? She was worried when she couldn't find you."

"Give me your pebbles," Dahl said and held out his hands. "I'll put them in your room."

Thor dumped his handful of rocks into Dahl's hands then sprinted off in search of his friend.

When he was out of earshot, Dahl asked, "What happened to Matilda?"

"She fainted after not eating her breakfast." Kyle started walking to the stable door. "Do you know what's wrong with her? Selby's been vague."

"I think that's because the doctors aren't sure." Dahl dropped the pebbles back in his pocket. "It started during the war, I think. Teigen was told she needed to eat more meat, so he put chickens in the chapel and a pigsty in the woods to keep the Nazis from finding them and confiscating them."

"But that ended five years ago," Kyle said slowly.

"Exactly. And Matilda has not gotten better."

The pair walked across the courtyard. "Poor Nikolai," Kyle murmured. "You can tell how much he loves her."

"In my opinion, that's the only reason she's still with us."

Dahl opened the back door of the house and waited for Kyle to go through first. Since the war ended and Teigen moved back to Arendal with Selby, he'd continually expressed his concern for his mother's health.

And since the christening of little Jans, Matilda spent most of her days out of sight, only joining her family and guests at supper. Even then, she never ate much.

"Should we go upstairs or wait down here?" he asked Kyle.

"I think maybe you should wait down here." She looked up

the staircase. "But I'm going up."

Dahl pulled her close and kissed her softly. "We'll talk later, after we hear what the doctor says."

⚡ ⚡ ⚡

Teigen sat beside his mother's bed and held her hand. "What can I do for you, Mamma?"

She gazed at him. "I want to talk to Kyle."

"Are you sure you're up to that?" he asked softly. "Don't you want to rest?"

She tried to squeeze his hand and the attempt was so pitiful Teigen's chest tightened.

"I have to talk to Kyle," she repeated.

Teigen turned his head when he heard footsteps and he was relieved to see Kyle entering the room. "Here she is, Mamma."

He motioned Kyle forward and gave her his chair. "She wants to talk to you."

"Me?" Kyle looked surprised as she sat. She faced Matilda. "What is it, Mamma Hansen?"

Teigen turned around to leave the room, but his mother stopped him. "I want you to hear what I say."

"Okay, Mamma." Teigen stood at the end of the bed.

Matilda felt for Kyle's hand and Kyle took hold of Matilda's thin hands with both of hers.

She leaned forward. "Talk to me."

"First, I am so glad Tor found you." Matilda's voice was breathy. "You gave my son happiness in his last months of his life."

"I loved him very much, Mamma."

"I know you did. And you gave him a strong beautiful son." Matilda sighed. "At least part of him lives on for us."

Kyle looked at Teigen, her expression wistful. There was really nothing for her to say.

"But now..." Matilda paused and drew two deep breaths. "Now you have to marry again. This is my wish for you and for Thor."

Kyle smiled. "I will."

"Now. Not later." Matilda urged. "Don't wait too long. Thor is getting too old."

Kyle turned to Teigen and motioned him to her side. "What should I say?" she whispered in his ear.

That was a very good question.

As much as Teigen wanted to believe that his mother's health was going to improve, he's seen her slow steady decline over the last year. Whatever she suffered from was finally defeating her.

"Tell her what she wants to hear," he whispered back. "I don't know if she'll be with us long enough to see if it happens."

Kyle gasped quietly and her eyes met his. "Oh, Teigen…"

He stepped back, willing himself not to cry. "Go on."

Kyle faced Matilda again. "I *am* going to get married, Mamma. Soon."

"I'm so glad…" She closed her eyes and then opened them again. "Who are you marrying?"

Kyle shot a nervous glance at Teigen, her expression uncertain.

He nodded his encouragement.

"I'm going to marry," she pulled a breath then said, "Dahl Holter."

"Dahl?" Matilda smiled a little. "I like him. He's an actor, you know."

"I do know that."

"He's very handsome." Matilda waved a weak hand. "Don't tell Nikolai I said that."

Kyle smiled. "I won't."

"When?"

"As soon as you're strong enough to be there, Mamma."

Matilda's smile disappeared. "Don't wait for that, Kyle."

Teigen stepped forward. "Mamma?"

"Get your father."

"Why?"

Kyle jumped up from the chair. "You sit. I'll get him."

ᚾ ᚾ ᚾ

Kyle ran down the stairs. "Nikolai? Selby!"

Dahl and Nikolai came out of the Great Hall and Selby rushed from the kitchen wing.

"Is it Matilda?"

Kyle nodded and got out of the way as Nikolai and Selby hurried up the steps.

Dahl grabbed her hand. "Is she gone?"

"No." Kyle started back up the stairs pulling Dahl behind her. "But you need to come, too."

ᚾ ᚾ ᚾ

Matilda Sorensen Hansen passed to her reward that same evening, surrounded by her loving family. Thor and Torhild were allowed to see her before Gjertrud bathed them and put them to bed. Tomorrow morning their parents would explain to them that their grandmother had gone to heaven and they wouldn't see her anymore.

Kyle sat beside her sleeping son and her heart ached that he'd lost his grandmother before he even got to know her.

"So much loss for a little boy," she whispered.

Dahl knocked on the door frame. "I came to say goodnight."

Kyle stood. "I'll come down for a while. I can't sleep yet."

She and Dahl descended the stairs together. In the Great Hall, Dahl poured her a glass of wine and himself a tumbler of aquavit. She sat on the sofa, kicked off her shoes, and tucked her feet under her.

"Some day, huh?"

Dahl sat next to her. "That's putting it mildly."

She took a sip of the wine and stared at the flames in the fireplace. "She told me to get married soon."

"Did she?"

Kyle looked at Dahl. "Teigen told me to say I *was* getting married soon. Then she asked to whom."

Dahl gave her an adorably crooked smile. "Did my name come up?"

"Well I thought about telling her I was marrying Frank Sinatra..." Kyle shrugged. "Then I realized I had a much better possibility right here in Arendal."

Dahl set his drink on the low table. "I think we need to make our situation official."

He took Kyle's glass and set it on the table beside his. Then he held her hands and stared into her eyes.

"I love you, Kyle. I can't believe I'm saying this after knowing you for just a couple weeks, but you have moved into my heart and made yourself at home."

Kyle squeezed his hands. "And I love you, Dahl Holter. I have no explanation for it either. But the way you spoke to Thor today solidified it for me."

Dahl nodded. "So the crucial question will have to wait until three things to happen."

Kyle frowned. "What three things?"

"First, when I take Thor shooting tomorrow, I'm going to ask his permission to marry you."

"What if he says no?"

Dahl chuckled. "He won't. Next, I have to buy a ring."

Kyle felt for the gold band inlaid with three small diamonds that she wore on a chain around her neck. When she was officially engaged it would be time to take Tor's ring off and put it in safekeeping until Thor was old enough to have it.

"What's the third thing?" she whispered.

"I want to wait until after Matilda's funeral."

Kyle approved. "That's very thoughtful, Dahl."

That's him, Kyle.

Kyle smiled at Tor's words this time, certain that soon she would never need to hear them again.

CHAPTER TEN

July 21, 1950

Matilda's funeral service was attended by the majority of the population in Arendal and Kyle realized what a large part of the town the Hansen family actually was. Even Olina made the journey back from Bergen, though Kyle was certain she had more than one purpose in returning to Arendal.

The size of the gathering made her wonder what the impact of Teigen's planned sale of Hansen Shipping would be. Just because the company was sold didn't mean it would stop operations here.

But it might. Did that mean dozens of townspeople would lose their jobs?

While Kyle thought the possible sale was confidential information, apparently Nikolai didn't. She overheard several men discussing it, assuming the American in their midst didn't understand them. All of a sudden, she grasped Tor's viewpoint.

It can *be helpful if they don't know.*

She made it a point to listen to the conversations around her, gleaning what she could. The concerns expressed about the sale of the company were quite vehement. She'd need to talk to Teigen about that on another day.

Not the day he buried his mother.

Selby stayed by Nikolai's side as the funeral guests filled the Great Hall. Her father-in-law looked sad, of course, but there was an air of peace in his presence. Watching the woman he loved so dearly fade away from him over the last decade had obviously been extremely hard. To have her suffering come to a peaceful end was a blessing.

Mrs. Nilssen had been cooking for the last five days and the expansive table in the dining room was laden with every traditional Norwegian dish that Kyle was familiar with—and many that she wasn't.

After the church service and the graveside goodbyes, Thor and Torhild were excused from the somber adult gathering at Hansen Hall. Gjertrud took them back into town for ice cream and to play in the park until suppertime.

Olina stuck to Dahl like a tick on a deer.

Kyle watched him try to extricate himself from her presence without luck. Only when he excused himself to use the lavatory did she wander off to talk to her grieving uncle.

When Dahl returned, he leaned over and whispered *help me* in Kyle's ear.

She laughed. "Do you want me to use a choke hold? I'm out of practice but I might be able to manage it."

Dahl smiled down into her eyes. "I adore you."

And then he kissed her.

It was a quick but solid kiss on her lips, with just enough hesitation that it couldn't be called a peck. Dahl was sending Olina a message.

"Can I get you something?" he asked.

"Coffee with cream? And some of those almond cookies?"

"I'll be right back." When Dahl walked toward the dining room Kyle risked a glance toward Olina.

If looks were lethal, she'd be joining her mother-in-law in short order.

When the crowd gradually diminished, final condolences were given and accepted, and only the family—including Olina—remained, they rested in the scattered chairs strewn through the Great Hall.

"It was a beautiful day," Nikolai stated. "Matilda would have been completely embarrassed by such a show."

"It was what she deserved, Pappa." Teigen's smile was sad. "Mamma was a special woman."

"And strong," Selby added. "She survived longer than any of the doctors thought she would."

"She wanted to meet Kyle and Thor." Nikolai turned to look at Kyle. "You made her so happy, daughter. She was at peace with Tor's death at last."

Kyle smiled softly. "I am so glad to have come here. And for so many reasons, I can't begin to count them."

Dahl came into the Great Hall with Thor in tow. Her son's hair was damp from his bath and he had his pajamas on. And he smiled at Kyle like he was about to burst.

Kyle set her coffee aside, glad for Dahl's thoughtfulness. "Coming to say goodnight, sweetheart?"

Thor ran to her. He climbed into the chair and squeezed himself next to her. Kyle put her arm around him and kissed the top of his head.

Dahl was standing in front of her.

Kyle looked up at him. Her pulse sped up when she saw the loving expression on his face.

"I have a question to ask you, Kyle Solberg Hansen."

Little gasps bounced through the room as Dahl knelt in front of Kyle and Thor. Kyle was suddenly shaking and tears blurred her vision.

Why do I always cry so easily?

Dahl held up a box with a sparkling diamond ring in it. "Will you marry me, Kyle?" He asked first in Norsk, and then repeated the question in English for Thor's sake.

Olina let out a little cry.

Thor tapped Kyle's shoulder. "Say yes, Mamma. Then Dahl can come to America and live with us."

"Thor already said yes, Kyle." Dahl reached for her left hand. "Will you?"

Kyle looked around the room. Teigen and Selby were holding hands and grinning. Nikolai gazed at her, clearly not surprised. Judging by his wistful expression he was probably remembering the moment when he proposed to Matilda.

Ben, who had returned from Oslo for the funeral of his adopted grandmother, moved to stand by Olina and slipped a comforting hand around her waist while he winked at Kyle.

"Mamma?" Thor prompted. "Say yes."

Kyle looked at her son, a carbon copy of his father. "I just want to remember this, Thor. Because I'm so happy."

She kissed his head again and looked at Dahl. "I never thought I'd find love again, but I was wrong. Yes, Dahl Holter, I will marry you without any hesitation or reservation."

Thor let out a little whoop.

Dahl slid the ring on her finger and pulled her to her feet. This time his kiss left her breathless.

July 22, 1950

Kyle and Dahl stayed up until the sun rose at four o'clock, dividing the hours between talking about what they needed to do before Kyle left Norway in eleven days, and taking advantage of the privacy of the firelight and empty Hall to physically express their love and attraction.

While they remained fully clothed, their apparel didn't hamper the sensual exploration that their newly cemented status encouraged. Kyle snuggled into Dahl's embrace, contentment flooding her veins.

"Let's go over it one more time," she murmured. "Tomorrow we get the marriage license and make arrangements with the church."

"Right. And whatever other details need to be taken care of here in Arendal." Dahl moaned a happy-sounding sigh. "Photographer, flowers, whatever needs to be ordered."

"Then you'll head for Oslo the next morning to take care of theater stuff." Kyle knew she would miss him, but he was only going to be gone from Arendal one night.

"I think Gunter Salversen will do a great job in my place, and I know he's eager for the chance to take over." Dahl kissed her forehead. "I hope you'll get a chance to meet him."

"Maybe when we fly out." Kyle didn't want to think about that at the moment. "What day will you try to get your ticket for?"

"I think I'll need at least five days to go back to Bergen, go through my stuff and pack it up, then head back to Oslo for the flight."

Dahl had suggested, and Kyle agreed, that it made more sense for the two of them to spend as much time as possible together while she and Thor were still here, and then get himself sorted and packed after she left.

"It's only five days," she said for her own sake. "And that gives me time to get the house ready—and let Beth know she needs to move into the other half of the duplex."

"My passport is current, since I renewed it to go to Iowa two years ago."

Another tip-off that Dahl spoke English. Kyle couldn't believe she'd missed that.

"Which brings me to my next point." Dahl shifted so he could see her face. "I wrote to Iowa State University a week ago and enquired about the position they offered me. I asked them to reply to me at your address."

So many parts of that statement surprised Kyle. "How'd you get my address?"

"From Teigen."

"But why have them reply to me?" she asked. "What if you stayed in Norway?"

Dahl huffed a little laugh. "Then their answer wouldn't matter, would it?"

"I guess not..." Kyle brushed her hair out of her eyes. "Have we forgotten anything?"

"Just money, but I can't do anything about that yet." Dahl wove his fingers between Kyle's. "Once I set up a bank account in America I'll have my savings wired there."

"Ooh. Am I marrying a wealthy man?" Kyle teased.

"Probably not. But I'm far from destitute." Dahl lifted their entwined hands to his lips and kissed her fingers. "And for a professional actor, that's actually quite an accomplishment."

"I wonder what will happen when Teigen sells Hansen

Shipping," Kyle mused. "I overheard some men talking about it earlier and they didn't sound happy."

Dahl's brow puckered. "Did you tell Teigen?"

Kyle made a disbelieving face. "No. Not at his mother's funeral."

"Oh—right." Dahl shook his head. "That seems like days ago already."

"It does." Kyle reluctantly pushed herself up from the sofa. "And speaking of days, the sun is up."

Dahl stretched and yawned. "If we go to bed now we might be able to get five hours of sleep before we start working through our list of things to do."

Kyle held out her hand, Dahl grabbed it, and she pulled him to his feet. "Walk me home?"

"With pleasure." He engulfed her in his arms for one long, last kiss, ending with a heavy sigh. "How many days until we're married?"

July 24, 1950

The answer turned out to be four.

I'm getting married tomorrow.

Dahl drove back toward Arendal and waited for the panic prompted by that thought to set in. When it didn't appear, he pushed harder.

I'm marrying a woman I've only known for three weeks.

Still nothing.

True, they'd been together constantly during that time and had talked about every conceivable subject he could think of. Dahl felt like Kyle knew him better than possibly his parents did at this point.

And he knew enough about her and her story to respect her strength, intelligence, and determination. She'd faced heart-breaking loss and triumphed over it with dignity and love.

The fact that she was absolutely gorgeous with her thick blonde hair and intriguing gray-green eyes—which he noticed changed with her moods—only made the prospect of spending his life with her that much more appealing.

Dahl tested the panic one last time.

I'm moving to America in two weeks.

Dahl smiled. Gunter was pretty happy about that.

Sergeant Gunter Salversen was the second male lead and accountant for the Royal Shakespearean Acting Troupe, their cover for Milorg resistance activities during the war. When the war ended and Dahl started directing plays as well as acting in them, he and Gunter reconnected.

Gunter was a talented actor and he had aspirations similar to Dahl's. So when Dahl told Gunter what he was planning to do, Gunter didn't seem to know how to react.

"Really? You're leaving?" Gunter looked stricken. "What about the production in Oslo?"

"It's all yours if you want it." Dahl shook Gunter's shoulder. "And I'm hoping you do."

"Just like that? I'm the director?" Gunter was clearly trying not to look happy. "And you're off to America?"

"Please say yes, my friend," Dahl urged. "I want to leave everything in good hands."

"And your future contracts?"

"All yours."

Gunter did smile at that point. "My wife is going to kiss your feet."

Relief. "Is that a yes?"

It was. And when Dahl took Gunter to the theater and explained that even though he was leaving, the production would be in very good hands, the theater manager finally agreed to accept the change of command and not sue Dahl for breach of contract.

I'll be in America, anyway.

Still no fear.

Oddly the one thing he wasn't even slightly worried about was being Thor's father. Though he believed that responsibility would strike fear in the hearts of most other men, Dahl really liked the boy. And after taking him shooting a few times, Thor decided he liked Dahl.

Kyle's son needed a strong, kind man in his life to guide

him, and Dahl was honored to be that man. And when he and Kyle had children of their own, Thor would be a very helpful big brother.

Dahl glanced at the packet on the car's passenger seat that held his plane tickets. He visited the ticket agent yesterday and the man called the airlines to make his reservations: Bergen to Oslo, Oslo to New York, New York to Minneapolis.

This morning he'd picked up the handwritten tickets and the typed itinerary. He would board the first flight on August sixth, and land in Minneapolis on the seventh. Dahl sighed happily.

I can't wait.

※ ※ ※

Teigen led the four men who asked to meet with him into the office where his father and his father's father and countless men before that had run Hansen Shipping. He wasn't sure why they asked for this meeting, but he was pretty sure it had to do with his plan to sell the company.

Teigen heard his father talking about it during the gathering at Hansen Hall following his mother's funeral. While Teigen believed the possibility was a secret, Nikolai clearly thought that the town needed to know.

"They sounded really angry," Kyle said the next day when she told him about the conversations she'd overheard. "I thought you should know."

Teigen thanked her sincerely. He was glad he wouldn't be blindsided if a protest arose.

It looked like that was exactly what he was facing today.

"Have a seat, gentlemen." Teigen pulled two additional chairs in front of the massive desk. "Would you like coffee?"

"Yes. Thank you," one answered for the group.

Teigen asked the office secretary to bring something to nibble on along with the five coffees and then took his place at the desk. "Now, what can I do for you?"

The man who answered the coffee question leaned forward. "We want to buy Hansen Shipping."

CHAPTER ELEVEN

"They formed a cooperative," Teigen explained at supper that night. "They gathered some of the supervisors together and they want to buy Hansen Shipping."

Kyle thought that was brilliant. She just had one question. "How will they pay for it?"

"They put together a decent amount of money to put down—about ten percent of the value of the business," Teigen said. "They want to pay the rest off over ten years."

"What did you tell them?" Selby asked.

Teigen looked at his wife. "I said I had to talk it over with Kyle."

"What?" Kyle looked at Teigen in shock. "Why me?"

That question seemed to surprise her brother-in-law. "Because Thor will receive his father's portion of the family business if I sell the company, of course."

Kyle looked at Dahl. "Did you know this?"

Her fiancé nodded. "I did. I'm surprised you didn't."

Kyle slid an accusing look at Teigen. "Why didn't you tell me?"

Teigen still looked surprised. "I thought it was obvious."

And it should have been, Kyle realized. "I guess I just never thought about it."

"Well think about it now," Teigen said gently. "It would mean an income for Thor for the next ten years."

"Money that could be invested, Kyle," Dahl added. "So when he's old enough he could pay for college or maybe a buy a house."

A terrible, horrible, frightening thought reared up. "Is that why you want to marry me?" she asked Dahl. "So you can manage Thor's money?"

Dahl looked like she'd punched him. "Of course not."

"To be honest, Kyle, that was one of the reasons we're so happy about your marriage," Teigen offered. "Selby and I trust Dahl to make sure Thor gets every penny that's due him."

"As opposed to some random American?" she spat. Why that made her angry she had no idea.

Selby leaned forward. "Surely you can understand that concern, Kyle."

Selby's soft tone had the effect of a warm blanket wrapping around her. Kyle leaned back in her chair and tried to make sense of her unexpected emotions.

"Kyle?"

She turned to Dahl, wary of what he might say. "What?"

"I have plenty of money on my own. And I understand how to invest to make that money earn interest." He laid his hand over hers. "If you don't want me to touch Thor's inheritance, I'll leave the management completely up to you."

Kyle looked into his beautiful blue eyes. "Thank you."

Dahl moved his attention to Teigen. "What interest rate will you charge them?"

Teigen shrugged. "I was thinking five percent of the remaining balance per year."

Dahl seemed to approve. "Would you wire the money to Kyle on a regular basis?"

"I was thinking quarterly."

Dahl faced Kyle again who was listening carefully to the exchange. She never would have thought to ask any of those questions, and was so glad that Dahl did. "You can set up a special account and keep Thor's money separate from our income."

Kyle nodded slowly and wondered why she doubted him. She wanted to slap herself at the moment. She deserved it.

"That's a very good idea, Dahl. We can talk about investing it later, when the payments actually start coming." She squeezed his hand. "I'm sorry. I guess I'm more stressed than I realized."

He smiled and her heart lifted. "Understandable."

Kyle looked at Teigen again. "Do you want to accept the offer?"

"I do." He glanced at his father who sat silently at the head of the table. "It would assure that Hansen Shipping stays in Arendal and the men who work for us will still have jobs."

"I agree," Nikolai said quietly.

"Then so do I," Kyle said confidently. "But can I suggest one addition to the negotiations?"

One corner of Teigen's mouth lifted. "What would that be?"

"Keep a piece of the company. Maybe only ten percent." Kyle smiled at Nikolai. "To honor centuries of Hansens at the helm."

"I like it." Teigen turned to Selby. "What do you think?"

"I agree," she answered. "But I'd also add that a Hansen sits on the cooperative's board."

Teigen's shoulders slumped. "I don't have time for that. Or the desire, to be honest."

Selby lifted one eyebrow. "Who says it has to be you?"

Teigen's eyes rounded. "You?" he blurted.

"Why not?" she challenged. "It's the nineteen fifties and women are doing all sorts of things like that. Look at Kyle. She might be getting a Ph.D. in psychology."

Teigen turned wide eyes to Dahl. "Do you hear this?"

Kyle pointed a finger at Teigen. "What we women did during the war made certain that the right side won. You know that's true."

Dahl's mouth opened and closed. Clearly he couldn't deny her words.

"And because of those experiences some of us aren't content to just disappear into kitchens and diapers," Kyle continued. "We want to share your burdens. Share your world."

"She makes a good point, Teig," Dahl admitted. "And so does Selby."

"I agree with keeping ten percent of the company." Teigen gazed at his father. "Pappa? Do you agree that I should let Selby sit on the board?"

Nikolai smiled a little. "Your mother would have agreed. So I must."

"All right, then. I'll accept the offer and set up the sale of ninety percent of Hansen Shipping." Teigen's eyes twinkled mischievously. "And I'll let them know that Mrs. Selby Hansen will be sitting on their board of directors.

He chuckled. "God help them!"

July 25, 1950

Dahl and his best man Teigen left for the church first, holding to the tradition of the groom not seeing his bride until she appeared at the end of the aisle at the beginning of the ceremony.

Selby shooed the men from the house at nine o'clock, a full hour before the scheduled nuptials, so they opted to walk into town and get a cup of coffee in the meantime.

The wedding would be small because both Dahl and Kyle were visitors to Arendal, but Dahl had called friends in Bergen and Oslo to invite them to the sudden event. Kyle had no idea if any of them would be able to make it to the mid-week morning wedding, but she doubted it.

Last night as she was packing for their two-night honeymoon, she explained what was happening to Thor. "We'll go to the church and have the wedding at ten o'clock. After that, we'll go to that restaurant you like and have a big lunch."

"Can I have dessert?" he asked.

"You can have whatever you want," Kyle promised. "After we're done, Uncle Teigen will bring you back to the house while Dahl and I take a little trip."

Thor scowled. "Where are you going?"

"To a town about half-an-hour south of here, called

Grimstad. We're staying there for two nights." Kyle straightened and rubbed her lower back. "It's what people do when they get married."

Thor didn't look convinced. "Why?"

Kyle thought of the real reason and a thrill of anticipation snaked through her gut. "It's a chance for the new husband and wife to spend some time alone."

"Why?"

"Because after the wedding, they need some time alone."

"Why?"

Kyle floundered for an explanation her five-year-old son would understand. "Because... they want to kiss. A lot."

Thor wrinkled his nose. "When I marry Torhild will I have to kiss her a lot?"

Kyle bit back her smile and gave Thor an empathetic look. "Oh, sweetie. You can't marry Torhild. She's your cousin."

That was startling news to Thor. "But I love her."

"I know you do. And when you get older, you'll find another girl to love." Kyle opened a drawer and lifted the armful of clothes stored there. "Do you want to help me move my clothes?"

"Where're you putting them?"

"In Dahl's room. That's where I'll be sleeping when we get back." Kyle flashed her happiest smile, hoping to convince Thor to be happy, too. "You'll have this room all to yourself! Won't that be nice?"

Thor looked like the floor was crumbling beneath him. "No."

"Think about it—you can stay up and look at your books as long as you want to," Kyle cajoled. "Besides, after we get back from Grimstad it's only for five more nights. After that, we fly back home."

Thor accepted the stack of sweaters Kyle handed him with a grunt, but he helped her move her clothes without further complaint.

Kyle looked at Selby in the mirror when her sister-in-law pinned a final curl in place. "I'm going to miss you when we leave."

"I'm going to miss you, too." Selby rested her hands on

Kyle's shoulders and met her gaze in the glass. "Please promise me you'll come back."

"I'll have to. Thor will need to check on his holdings." Kyle grinned. "And you know the planes do fly in both directions. You all should come visit us in Minnesota."

"Visit America?" Selby looked surprised by the idea. "Maybe we should."

She stepped back. "You look amazing, Kyle."

Kyle turned around and rose to her feet. Being a widow with a child precluded her wearing white, but the cream-colored light wool suit and veiled hat she purchased yesterday were beautifully tailored. "I hope Dahl thinks so."

"How could he not?" Selby looked at her own reflection and smoothed her short hair before pinning her hat in place. "Are you ready?"

"More than you know," Kyle admitted. "Let's go."

N N N

Dahl was surprised to see a dozen of his friends enter the church and take their place on his side of the aisle. Gunter and his wife, Karolina Ingebrigtsen, who had been Selby's understudy, sat grinning in the pews. Bennett Wilhelmsen, their erstwhile props manager, was there with his wife. The couples chattered happily, reuniting while they waited for the ceremony to begin.

Only Ben sat on Kyle's side, but he had also brought a guest. The young woman was dressed in very modern clothing and carried herself with an artistic flair. Dahl understood the attraction immediately.

A flurry of activity at the back of the church drew Dahl's attention. The pastor walked up to him and suggested the men get in place.

"This is it," Teigen teased. "Last chance to escape."

"Shoot me if I try," Dahl teased back. "Because I will clearly have lost my mind."

The door to the narthex opened and Selby, Kyle's matron of honor, appeared. Grinning like a fool and carrying a bouquet of pink roses, she walked forward in time with the music while the organist played *Pachelbel's Canon in D.*

When she took her place at the front of the church, the organist switched to *Wedding Day at Troldhaugen* by the Norwegian composer Edvard Grieg. All heads in the little crowd swiveled to the back of the church.

When Kyle stepped into view, Dahl thought he was dreaming. How could such an incredible woman have fallen in love with him? He was nothing special. Not compared to her.

Kyle's eyes met his and hers were glittering with her normal tears. Her tender heart made him love her even more.

Thor, in a brand-new suit and tie, took his role seriously and concentrated on stepping in tandem with his mother as he held her hand and walked her down the aisle.

Once they reached the adults in the front of the church, Thor sat in the first pew with Ben while Dahl and Kyle faced the pastor.

When the cleric asked, "Who gives this woman to be married?"

Thor stood up.

"I do," he said loudly. Then he sat down and beamed at his mother. "You can get married now, Mamma."

N N N

Kyle pushed her plate away. "I can't eat another bite."

"When do you want to leave?" Dahl asked quietly.

"How about fifteen minutes ago?" Kyle was only half teasing. "Are you ready?"

Dahl looked down the table of assembled friends and family members. "I am. Let me offer one last toast."

Dahl stood and raised his glass of champagne. When he had everyone's attention, he said, "Thank you all for coming today, in spite of the short notice. My wife and I could not be happier."

He smiled down at Kyle. "And now we are going to leave you to your continued celebration, and head out. *Skål!*"

Dahl gulped the last bit of champagne in his glass, then set it down and grabbed Kyle's hand.

"We'll see you in two days," he said to Thor. "And don't worry, I'll take very good care of your mother. I promise."

Dahl was a man of his word.

The inn in Grimstad was charming. The view of the North Sea from their room was gorgeous. The bed was oversized and the down-filled comforters felt like clouds. The fireplace burned away dampness and kept the room cozy.

That was good, because once she got past her initial shyness, Kyle and Dahl spent the rest of the day and night buck naked.

Anticipation of her wedding night had weighed on Kyle for the two days that Dahl was gone to Oslo. Tor was the only man she'd ever disrobed in front of, and the only man she'd ever had sex with. She didn't expect to have to go through this process again with a different man.

While her previous experience should make her feel more confident, the opposite was actually true.

Would Dahl be physically different from Tor? Would he want to make love the same way Tor did? Would she be as responsive as she was six years ago?

Had she forgotten how to do it altogether?

Dahl had noticed her nervousness and asked her about it.

"I'm not sure I remember what to do," she confessed.

Dahl ran his fingers through her hair dislodging Selby's carefully placed hairpins. "It's not something you forget, darling. Trust me, will you?"

Kyle shook out her hands trying to discharge her nerves. "At least I know it won't hurt."

"Not at all. Far from it." Dahl pulled her head forward and claimed her lips.

Just like Dahl's kisses dispelled thoughts of Tor's so did his lovemaking.

With only a couple weeks to enjoy their marriage, Tor loved her robustly and as frequently as they could be together. He left her breathless and quivering each time, but time was never a luxury they had.

Dahl acted like they had all the time in the world. He roused her tenderly, touching and kissing her in ways Kyle never imagined, until she begged him to get to the point before she died from desire.

He did.

Kyle writhed under him, pushing to get him closer, deeper, until there was no space left. Her entire existence coalesced into a tingling ball of energy which exploded magnificently, throwing her outside of her body into the ether.

When she drifted back into earth's atmosphere, she heard Dahl's grunts and growls as he was claimed by his own consuming culmination. When he stopped trembling, he looked her in the eyes, panting over her and looking euphoric.

"My God, Kyle..." he rasped.

Kyle pulled him into a kiss. Her legs were still wrapped around his hips and he was still inside her. She didn't want either of them to move.

When the kiss ended, she was crying.

"I'm so happy," she snuffled. "I love you so much."

Dahl kissed her tears away. "I love you, Kyle. You have no idea how much."

She smiled softly. "Will you show me again?"

CHAPTER TWELVE

July 28, 1950

Kyle held Dahl's hand as they sat in Teigen's office. She couldn't stop touching him; it seemed she was afraid that if she let go he would disappear.

Her first love did.

Dahl knew that while he would never live in Tor's shadow, he would have to live in the detritus of the man's untimely death. At least for a while.

Dahl squeezed Kyle's hand and winked at her. *I love you*, he mouthed.

She beamed happily and her cheeks pinkened.

Moving into his bedroom last night went more smoothly than he anticipated. Kyle had already explained the situation to Thor, but the boy was still not happy about it. So Dahl took a shot at helping the five-year-old understand.

He didn't play fair. "Do you want a brother or sister?"

Thor looked skeptical. "Yes…"

If Thor hadn't had so much fun with Torhild over the month, Dahl wasn't sure he would have given that same answer, but this gamble had clearly paid off.

"Well then, the mamma and pappa need to sleep in the same

bed, without anyone else in the room, so a baby can grow in the mamma's tummy."

And that was that. Thor was on board with the arrangement.

Of course, he did ask them at breakfast this morning if the baby was growing yet. Neither he nor Kyle were surprised, considering Dahl's explanation.

"We won't know until Halloween," Kyle told Thor. "Maybe not until Thanksgiving. Or even Christmas."

The boy frowned a little. "That's too long."

"Babies take a year," Kyle shrugged. "Sometimes longer."

Dahl grinned at Kyle. "Maybe we should take some naps together. That might help."

Thor brightened. "Do that!"

Kyle punched his arm, but she was laughing.

"Here they are." Teigen held up a stack of papers. "This is the official offer from the Hansen Shipping Cooperative."

He handed them to Kyle. "You can see there that they've offered two-hundred-and-twenty-five thousand for ninety out of one hundred shares of the company."

Dahl looked over his wife's shoulder while she read the document.

"The down payment will be twenty-five thousand," Teigen continued. "Loan payments will be made annually on December first and include five percent interest on the unpaid balance before the payment is credited."

"Is there an end date to the loan?" Kyle asked.

"Not at this point. The way it's written, they pay whatever they can." Teigen looked at Dahl then back at Kyle. "What are your thoughts?"

Dahl held back, waiting to see what his wife would say.

"I think there needs to be a minimum payment every year," she said. "They are free to pay more at any time, but not less."

Teigen nodded. "I agree. I don't want this to go for more than ten years."

"You know the business, Teig," Dahl injected. "Can they afford to make payments of twenty-thousand a year?"

"They should be able to. And if they expand, they can pay more." Teigen faced Kyle. "Do you agree? Twenty thousand a year plus interest?"

Kyle gave him a one-shoulder shrug. "That sounds fair to me."

Teigen made notes on a pad of paper. "Me, too. I'll send them that counter-offer today."

"So what should Kyle expect in the way of payments?" Dahl asked.

Teigen looked at him. "I'm keeping the twenty-five thousand as an emergency fund in case they default on the payments, and I'll put it in an interest-paying account. If all goes well, we'll split it at the end of the loan."

He shifted his attention to Kyle. "But starting next year, I'll wire you ten thousand every December—or half if they pay more—plus half the interest."

"Perfect." Kyle's expression turned impish. "Did they agree to Selby being on the board?"

"They agreed to a Hansen," Teigen hedged. "I didn't specify *which* Hansen."

"It shouldn't matter," Dahl said. "Who knows what the business world will be like in ten years or so."

"That's true." Kyle offered Teigen her hand. "If the cooperative agrees to the minimum payment, then I agree with the rest of the arrangements."

Teigen shook her hand and flashed a wry smile. "I'm really going to miss you, Kyle."

August 1, 1950

Kyle and Thor watched while Dahl loaded their cases into the trunk of his sedan. At four o'clock in the morning the shifting sunrise was now over an hour away, but they needed to get to the Oslo airport in time for their ten o'clock flight to New York.

Teigen and Selby stood next to Kyle and Selby was dabbing her eyes.

Kyle faced her sister-in-law. "It's been quite a month, hasn't it? I had no idea how my life would change by coming here."

"It's a wonder, that's for sure," Selby agreed. "Please write to us often and let us know how you're doing."

"And I'll send pictures," Kyle promised. "You do the same."

"Cross my heart."

The women embraced and both were crying. Kyle finally let go of Selby and wrapped her arms around the man who no longer looked as much like Tor to her. Teigen was his own man in her experience now.

"I love you, Teigen," she murmured. "Thank you for everything."

"Thank you for telling me what you did about Tor." His voice was rough with emotion. "God bless you and Thor."

Kyle pulled away and looked at her new husband. "He is blessing us. More than I ever expected."

Teigen reached down and lifted Thor to his eye level. "Take care, son. Come back and see us again."

Thor nodded eagerly. "I will."

"We need to go," Dahl prompted.

Kyle wiped her eyes and gave Selby another quick hug. "Take care of Nikolai. Give him my love."

"Of course."

They reached the airport with an hour to spare so Dahl bought them breakfast. Then he sat with Kyle and Thor at the gate while they waited to board the plane. Kyle held his hand with both of hers while Thor played on the floor with the toy airplane Dahl just presented him with.

"I'll see you in six days," he reminded her. "You'll hardly have time to miss me."

"That's a lie. I miss you already," Kyle replied. "How will I be able to sleep until then?"

Dahl chuckled. "You've slept alone for nearly six years. I think you'll survive six nights.

Kyle leaned in for a kiss. "You're a heartless bastard, Dahl Holter," she whispered.

"I love you, Kyle Solberg Hansen Holter," he said before obliging her.

She sighed happily when the brief and public kiss ended. "Should I keep all those names?"

"That's up to you." He kissed her again. "But you better get going."

Kyle stood and held out her hand to Thor. "Come on, Thor time to get on the plane."

Thor clambered to his feet and threw his arms around Dahl's hips. "I love you, Pappa."

Surprised, Kyle met Dahl's suddenly misty gaze.

He smiled and wiped his eyes. "I love you, too, son. I'll see you soon."

EPILOGUE

September 20, 1951
Ames, Iowa

"I'm so glad this is the last time I'll have to drive to Minneapolis." Kyle collected their breakfast dishes and set them in the sink. "After I defend my thesis I'm finally finished."

"I'm just glad you still fit behind the steering wheel." Dahl stepped up behind her and slid his palms over her swelling belly. "How's our little one today?"

"Active." Kyle pushed a heel out from under her ribs. "Two more months seems like such a long time right now."

He kissed her neck. "I wish I could come with you."

"Me, too. But if you did, how would Thor get to school?" Kyle turned in her husband's arms and looped her arms around his neck. "Plus, you have auditions to hold while I'm gone."

"Blasted job," he teased.

Kyle tilted her head up for a kiss and Dahl heartily answered her request.

"Ewww." Thor made a face as he reentered the kitchen.

Dahl laughed and faced his stepson. "Teeth brushed?"

Thor nodded.

"Okay. Let's go." He gave Kyle a quick peck goodbye. "Drive safely, darling."

✄ ✄ ✄

The five-hour drive to Minneapolis through acres on acres of Iowa cornfields and Minnesota wheat fields always gave Kyle a chance to ponder anything that came to her mind.

Usually she used the time to ruminate on her thesis—comparing the effects of war on various soldiers who saw action, to see if there were consistent components which the field of psychology could address—but for some reason she couldn't keep her mind focused today.

Considering her defense of her findings was tomorrow morning at ten o'clock, that wasn't helpful.

Maybe because this is my last trip to the university as a student.

Over the last six years, Kyle had lived and breathed her studies. Until last summer's trip to Norway, of course, when her attentions were necessarily divided.

She smiled at the recollection of waiting at the Minneapolis airport for Dahl's arrival from Norway. Both of her parents were with her, astounded and unhappy that their daughter had once more gone off to somewhere strange and come home married to a man they'd never met.

"Really, Kyle," her mother grumbled over the telephone line. "I can't believe you did this to us again."

"It was never my plan, Mamma. I'm as surprised as you are, to be honest." Kyle lowered her voice. "But Thor adores him, and he adores Thor."

"That's not enough reason to marry someone you barely know."

"No it's not," Kyle agreed. "And if I hadn't fallen in love with him myself, I wouldn't have done it. But I did."

Her mother sighed pointedly. "Well, I guess it's too late now…"

"So will you come and meet him?"

And they did.

Kyle ran into Dahl's arms the minute she saw him. "You made it!"

Thor's arms wrapped around her legs and Dahl's.

"Pappa!" he yelped. "I'm glad you're here!"

Whether her mother's mood was changed by watching Thor's reaction to Dahl, or hearing him call his new stepfather *Pappa*, or experiencing the tall Norseman's undeniably handsome charm wasn't clear.

What was clear was Kylli's wide-eyed reaction to meeting Dahl Holter. "Oh. Hello."

Dahl leaned over and kissed Kylli's cheek. "It's a pleasure to meet you, Mrs. Solberg."

Then he extended a hand to Ole. "I apologize for not speaking to you before I married your daughter, Mr. Solberg. I hope you'll give us your blessing now."

"Um, yes." Ole shook Dahl's hand. "The boy seems to like you."

"And I like him." Dahl had one arm around Kyle's waist and the other rested on Thor's head. "I've been very blessed with my new family."

Kyle sighed.

Thor had been very impatient at first for a baby brother or sister to appear, but he was soon distracted by the fascinating experience of going to kindergarten and he stopped asking every morning if a baby was on the way. So in May when Kyle and Dahl told him he was going to be a big brother before Thanksgiving, he was ecstatic.

Feeling the baby kick was his favorite pastime at the moment. That, and crossing off days on the calendar until Kyle's due date.

Kyle was looking forward to spending the next two months focusing on their coming child. As a single mother attending the university on the G.I. Bill she didn't have that luxury when Thor was born six years ago. She planned to savor it this time.

September 21, 1951
Minneapolis, Minnesota

Kyle stayed in her former duplex with Beth, who now owned the Victorian dwelling, both because it cost her nothing to stay there and it was close to the campus. Beth was engaged to marry a butcher, and her daughter Greta—three years older than Thor—was very excited that the man had a daughter of his own and wanted to tell Kyle every detail about them.

Beth shooed Greta away with an apology. "She does like to talk."

"I'm glad you're both happy," Kyle said sincerely as she sank onto the edge of the welcoming guest bed. "I don't know what I would have done without your help all those years."

"You gave us a home when we didn't have many options," Beth countered. "We did for each other."

That phrase stuck in Kyle's mind as she entered the room and faced a panel of professors to justify the findings in her thesis. It seemed the perfect conclusion for her statistics.

We'll do for each other.

November 14, 1951
Ames, Iowa

Kyle took a deep breath and pushed as hard as her exhausted body could after fourteen hours of labor.

"The head's out," the doctor said. "Relax and let me work the shoulders out."

Kyle gasped and tried to go limp as the baby slid from her body. "What is it?"

"A girl!" the nurse beside her said happily. "And she's a big one."

A girl. Thor has a sister.

Kyle smiled and closed her eyes. Her name would be Matilda.

We have a daughter, Dahl.

THE HANSEN FAMILY TREE

Sveyn Hansen* (b. 1035 ~ Arendal, Norway)

***

Rydar Hansen (b. 1324 ~ Arendal, Norway)
Grier MacInnes (b. 1328 ~ Durness, Scotland)

Eryndal Bell Hansen (b. 1327 ~ Bedford, England)
Andrew Drummond (b. 1325 ~ Falkirk, Scotland)

***

Jakob Petter Hansen (b. 1485 ~ Arendal, Norway)
Avery Galaviz de Mendoza (b. 1483 ~ Madrid, Spain)

***

Brander Hansen (b. 1689 ~ Arendal, Norway)
Regin Kildahl (b. 1693 ~ Hamar, Norway)

***

Martin Hansen (b. 1721 ~ Arendal, Norway)
Dagne Sivertsen (b. 1725 ~ Ljan, Norway)

Reidar Hansen (b. 1750 ~ Boston, Massachusetts)
Kristen Sven (b. 1754 ~ Philadelphia, Pennsylvania)

Nicolas Hansen (b. 1787 ~ Cheltenham, Missouri Territory)
Siobhan Sydney Bell (b. 1789 ~ Shelbyville, Kentucky)

Stefan Hansen (b. 1813 ~ Cheltenham, Missouri)
Kirsten Hansen (b. 1820 ~ Cheltenham, Missouri)
Leif Fredericksen Hansen (b. 1809 ~ Christiania, Norway)

***

Tor Hansen (b. 1913 ~ Arendal, Norway)
Kyle Solberg (b. 1919 ~ Viking, Minnesota)
Dahl Holter (b. 1913 ~ Lillehammer, Norway)

Teigen Hansen (b. 1915 ~ Arendal, Norway)
Selby Hovland (b. 1914 ~ Trondheim, Norway)

***

*Hollis McKenna Hansen (b. Sparta, Wisconsin)

Kris Tualla is a dynamic, award-winning, and internationally published author of historical romance and suspense. She started in 2006 with nothing but a nugget of a character in mind, and has created a dynasty with The Hansen Series, and its spin-off, The Discreet Gentleman Series. Find out more at: www.KrisTualla.com

Kris is an active PAN member of Romance Writers of America, the Historical Novel Society, and Sisters in Crime, and was invited to be a guest instructor at the Piper Writing Center at Arizona State University.

"In the Historical Romance genre, there have been countless kilted warrior stories told. I say it's time for a new breed of heroes. Come along with me and find out why: **Norway IS the new Scotland!***"*